Lighting up Loveland

JOY SKYE

VINCI
BOOKS

Vinci Books

vinci-books.com

Published by Vinci Books Ltd in 2025

1

The EU GPSR authorised representative is Logos Europe, 9 rue Nicolas
Poussion, 17000 La Rochelle, France
contact@logoseurope.eu

MIX
Paper | Supporting
responsible forestry
FSC® C018072

FSC
www.fsc.org

Printed and bound in Great Britain by Clays Ltd, Elcograf S.p.A.

By Joy Skye

Sublime Retreats Romances

Corfu Capers

Clueless in Croatia

Falling in Florence

Summer in San Sebastian

Lighting up Loveland

Moonlight over Morocco

Prologue

From: peterwilliams@sublimeretreats.com
To: lsanchez@yahoo.com

Dear Ms Sanchez,

We are delighted to offer you the position of Events Coordinator at our premiere ski resort, Loveland, Colorado.

As you know, we pride ourselves on having the only resort that caters specifically to caring for and teaching the younger members of our club to ski, so their parents can relax and enjoy the holiday season. Alongside the resort manager and the children's entertainment team, you will be required to provide a program that will entertain and delight both children and parents alike.

The full terms of employment are in the attached contract, which we need signed and returned by the end of business hours tomorrow.

We look forward to welcoming you for the winter season.

Best regards,
Peter Williams
Sublime Retreats General Manager

Chapter One

Feeling ridiculous, Lola tried to follow her sister up the slippery slope. The effort required to move, the unfamiliar weight of her boots, and the awkwardness of the skis in her arms, caused her to sweat in the borrowed snowsuit. Pausing, she blew at some loose strands of dark hair that were sticking to her forehead. When that didn't work, she swiped at them angrily with a gloved hand, glaring at her sister's back.

'Are you sure this is a good idea?' she called out, hoping Natasha would see sense, and they could go back to the cabin they shared and curl up in front of the fire with some hot chocolate. Maybe read a book, or do anything else, in fact, other than learn how to ski.

'Come on, Lola,' her younger sister shouted over her shoulder as she sped ahead, making it look so easy and effortless. They may look alike, but their skill sets were apparently very different. 'You wanted this job, and part of it involves being able to at least stand upright for more than two seconds on those skis!'

Cursing at her sibling's enjoyment at her discomfort, Lola took another step forward, promptly slipping and ending up in a lurid pink heap in the snow. Swearing under her breath, she lay there for a moment, looking up at the brilliant blue sky dotted with puffy clouds, wondering if she had made an awful mistake in accepting this position. The sound of her sister's laughter floated back to her, and she pushed herself up on her elbows, ready to give her what for. At that moment, a tiny figure came whooshing past her. A child of no more than four or five slalomed down the hill and out of sight as if it were the most natural thing in the world.

Come on, Lola, you've got this, she told herself sternly and struggled back to her feet. When she finally made it up to the brow of the hill, her sister was calmly texting on her phone without a care in the world. Natasha glanced up, raising an eyebrow at her sweaty sister.

'About time. OK, all you need to do is stay upright and aim down there,' she said, pointing one of her poles down what seemed like a fantastically steep hill. The sunlight glinted off its sheer white surface, almost blinding her, the end nowhere in sight.

'Are you serious? I'm not sure if this is a good place for me to start my maiden voyage,' Lola said, her head spinning and fear pricking her skin as she contemplated the incline in front of her.

'It's the beginner's slope, where they start the kids!'

Another gaggle of brightly clad children came sailing past, calling to each other, their gleeful giggles echoing across the snow, as if to emphasise her point. They both watched as the group sailed past and out of sight.

'Look,' Natasha said, a little more kindly. 'I'll go first. All

4

you have to do is follow me. Just remember, shins forward, hands out, shoulders in front of your hips.'

And with that she was off, gliding down the hill, leaving Lola gaping after her, a frown creasing her brow.

'OK, then,' she muttered, trying to replicate the stance that Natasha had been drilling into her all morning. She gave a tentative push, but nothing happened. She tried again, a little harder this time, and felt herself start to move. Holding her breath for a moment, as the world started to move in the right direction, she let out a little whoop as she built up some speed, giving another push with her poles. Concentrating fiercely, she gave another, more forceful push, propelling her pace, hoping against hope to catch up with her sister and put an end to her gloating.

'I'm doing it!' she crowed to the world at large. *I don't know what I was worried about,* she thought as she gave another push. Visions of sweeping to a halt at the bottom of the slope with the impressive spray of snow that she had seen other skiers do floated across her brain as she began picking up speed. A slight lip in the terrain announced a steeper gradient and as she sailed over it, Lola realised she was in trouble as she landed at an awkward angle.

'Tash!' she called, 'Tash!' But her sister was already nearing the bottom of the run, and there was no way she could hear her. Lola became conscious that she was veering alarmingly off to one side, away from the path her sister had taken and towards a clump of unforgiving looking pine trees. *This is it. I'm gonna die,* she thought hysterically, giving up all efforts at trying to control her descent. *I'm gonna die in a borrowed, yucky, pink snowsuit, doing something I hate.*

As she neared the trees, she heard someone yelling. 'Look out! Wedge!' the voice called in alarm and she realised she had her eyes closed. They flew open just in time to see she was about to crash into someone, but not in time to do anything about it, even if she knew how.

The impact shook the breath out of her with an unattractive grunt; her impetus knocking them both over into a pile of snow. Lola landed on top of the poor, unfortunate soul who had been in her way, her arms splayed out, poles flying off in different directions. After a dizzying second or two, relief that she had stopped and appeared to be in one piece washed over her, and she mumbled into the chest of the snowsuit she was currently resting on.

'Oh my God, I'm so sorry.'

'*Tabarnak*! You stupid woman, what the hell do you think you are doing? You could have injured me!' the man snarled at her. She could feel the words vibrating through his chest.

A flash of indignation shot through her. 'Injured you? What about me? I could have died,' she snapped, raising her head to glare up at him. Her eyes had time to take in his stubbled jaw with a scar running along his cheek and the most incredible blue eyes she'd ever seen, before he turned his face away with a snort of derision. He started unceremoniously manhandling her to disentangle himself, muttering under his breath all the while.

'Don't be ridiculous,' he growled, his accent adding bite to the words as he pushed her roughly to one side before standing up and brushing himself off. 'The only thing you have injured is your pride. You should take more care of others!'

And with that, he strode off, leaving her wallowing like a beached turtle on its back, cursing the day she ever came to Loveland.

Chapter Two

Stomping back towards the base of the beginner's slope to meet his class, Luka swore at the world in general. Cursing inexperienced skiers, especially ones with pretty faces, and his lot in life. Being reduced to teaching children after everything he had worked for! He glanced back to check and saw that the woman that crashed into him was struggling to her feet. Satisfied, he turned his attention to the group of eager little faces that were watching him expectantly.

'*D'accord,*' he announced to the group after doing a quick head count. 'It looks like you have all made it to the bottom in one piece. Betty, stop pushing Jacob!'

'Tomorrow we will move up to the next level,' he announced. Then, ignoring their upraised faces clamouring for another run today, he walked off without a word towards his accommodation. Trying not to let the ever-present ache in his leg be visible in his stride, he followed the path that led to the staff housing. It was a group of cabins with either one or two bedrooms, set slightly above and away from the village, to give them some privacy when they weren't working.

Inside his log cabin, he stripped off, and limped into the bathroom and the shower cubicle, turning it on to its hottest setting, letting the steaming water work its magic. Towelling himself dry and then wrapping it around his waist, he went back into the open-plan living area. Pulling open a cupboard in the kitchenette, he grabbed a glass and filled it with water before downing a couple of painkillers and lay carefully on his couch, hoping to rest up for a few hours before the first obligatory 'drinks mixer' of the season. A loud rapping on his door startled him out of his doze a few minutes later, extracting an angry string of expletives as he carefully manoeuvred upright.

'What do you want?' he demanded, flinging the door open, taken aback by the blast of harsh cold air and the sight of Roger Albright, the resort manager, standing there beaming at him.

'Good afternoon, Luka, just checking in to see how your first day of teaching went?'

Roger was a very 'hands on' manager whose 'door was always open' to his staff. His niceness was infuriating and made Luka's skin crawl. Nobody could be that pleasant all the time, for God's sake!

'It went fine,' he retorted, staring down at Roger's permanently smiling face, wondering how to get rid of the annoying little man without being rude.

'That's great news, great news. A great start to what I hope to be Sublime Retreat's best winter season so far here in Loveland!'

Roger's other annoying habit was repeating himself, but his smile was unwavering under Luka's glare. He clapped his hands together. 'I look forward to seeing you at the mixer this evening.'

'I am a little unwell,' Luka growled, leaving the sentence hanging hopefully in the frosty air.

'Come, come. I'm sure you wouldn't want to miss tonight! It's always great fun and always a great way to get to know the rest of the team. We have some new members this season. I'm sure you want to join us in welcoming them?'

Worn down by the sheer force of the man's bonhomie, Luka smiled weakly. 'I will come for a little,' he conceded reluctantly, forcing himself to grant the man a smile.

'Excellent, excellent. It's the perfect opportunity for some pictures for our Instagram feed. See you at seven,' Roger grinned, twirling on his heels and practically skipping down the steps. Shaking his head, Luka closed the door thoughtfully. He knew he should be grateful for this job, but it was hard not to dwell on what might have been. What should have been and who should have shared it with him.

That evening found him duly present inside the hall that housed special events and the weekly drinks mixer. The new shirt he'd donned straight from the packet irritated his skin, aggravating him further and doing nothing to improve his mood. The large wooden building was in the middle of the village and had a stage at the far end and a bar set up to one side. Heading straight to get a drink to make this evening bearable, he ordered a scotch on the rocks and leaned back on the wall, watching as the room filled up with this week's guests in all their finery. The never-ending loop of cheery Christmas music was already making his head throb, and he decided he would just stay for one drink. All he had to do was make sure Roger saw him, and then he could sneak off, back to the sanctuary of his cabin.

'Mr Bouchard, Mr Bouchard!' exclaimed a girlish voice. 'Don't I look pretty?' demanded Betty, twirling around in front of him to show off her red dress.

'Sure,' he nodded down at her expectant face, unsure what else to say. If it didn't involve skiing, he found children arduous to talk to.

'Now, Betty, leave your lovely instructor alone,' purred the girl's mother, placing a manicured hand on his bicep and giving it an appreciative squeeze. 'I'm sure he has better things to do than chat with us girls,' she trilled, throwing her head back to laugh.

Uncomfortable at the attention, Luka scanned the room for rescue and spotted the unforgettable face of the woman who had crashed into him earlier. Maybe she was a guest here? He should probably apologise for his reaction earlier in that case. He didn't want to start out the season with a guest complaining about him.

Making his excuses to Betty and her cloying mother, he weaved his way through the throng. As he watched, the woman laughed at something her friend had said. Her entire face lit up, and he faltered, taken aback by how beautiful she was. Steeling himself, he edged into their space and cleared his throat to announce his presence. She turned and her face fell as she recognised him, and his heart sank a little.

'Excuse me, Miss,' he said. 'I think I might owe you an apology,'

Her brown eyes gazed seriously up at him, and her generous lips twitched as she arched an eyebrow. 'Might?' she queried sharply before taking a sip of her wine, casually maintaining eye contact. Luka shrank back slightly, thrown by the sudden, thunderous beating of his heart, but battled on.

'No, no. More definitely, I think. I mean, it was stupid to run into me like that, but I should have been more... How do you say? Gracious?'

She spat out her drink. A fine spray of red wine splattering up his crisp white shirt. 'Stupid? How dare you call me stupid?' she cried. 'It was an accident, you arrogant man, nothing more or less. You can take your apology and shove it where the sun doesn't shine!'

With that, she turned to her friend, grabbing her hand. 'Come on, Tash. Let's find someone pleasant to talk to!'

On closer inspection, her friend looked so similar she must be a relative he thought as he stared after her retreating form. Despite the circumstances, he couldn't help but admire the way she filled her dress. Her long, dark hair tumbled in waves down her back, bouncing with every step. Curves in all the right places and a delicious sway to her walk, even when she was angry. This was the first time a woman had caught his attention in a very long time.

Oh well, he thought to himself. After this week, I will never see her again, so I guess it doesn't matter. Looking down at his stained shirt, he realised he had the perfect excuse to leave and, checking that Roger was nowhere close by, scurried towards the exit.

Chapter Three

'The nerve of the man!' Lola ranted, as they walked away. 'How dare he call me stupid!'

'He didn't exactly call you stupid,' Natasha responded soothingly. 'He just said that running into him was stupid, which is fair enough,' she finished with a giggle as they stopped by an empty table.

'Thanks for the support,' Lola snapped back, angrily slurping at her drink. After the humiliation of her failed skiing attempt this morning and the worry about losing her job as a result, she really wasn't in the mood for grumpy men telling her she was stupid.

'You should be nice to him, you know?'

'Who?' Lola asked distractedly.

'Luka, the man you just spat your drink on.'

'Why on earth should I be nice to him?' she demanded, looking up at her sister curiously.

'Well, you want to learn how to ski, and he is the resident ski instructor. Seems like a no-brainer to me.'

'Oh, God, I didn't realise he works here. Awkward!'

Lola said, heat rising to her face. The knowledge that she would have to keep bumping into this guy for the next six months was mortifying. 'You could have mentioned that earlier, Tash.'

Her sister grinned. 'I was too busy laughing at your undignified tangle with our hunky, grumpy instructor to mention anything. I knew you'd figure it out, eventually. Strange he tried to apologise though. He's not known for niceties. Quite the opposite, actually.'

'That really doesn't surprise me,' Lola sighed, wondering if she could approach him again and ask about some lessons. Dismissing this possibility as untenable, she shook her head. 'No, I'll just have to keep on trying. Can you take me out again tomorrow, sis?'

'No can do, I'm afraid. I'll be working all day. You should reconsider talking to Luka about lessons, I think he's your best bet. Head's up, here comes our esteemed leader,' she said, nodding over at Roger who was making his way towards them, meeting and greeting everyone in his path with a smile and an encouraging word.

'The lovely Sánchez sisters!' he declared. 'How are we this evening? And Lola, welcome, welcome to the team. Are you settling in?' He was bouncing on his toes, positively vibrating with good intentions.

'We are fine, and yes I am. Thank you, Roger. I need to set up a meeting with you. I have some great ideas for some new events over the next few weeks that I wanted to discuss?'

'Excellent, excellent,' Roger beamed. 'Fresh blood, fresh ideas, huh? Although, the main event will always be the Christmas extravaganza, of course. The sight of all our staff sweeping down the slope in their costumes every week in December is always the highlight of the holiday season.'

Trying to match Roger's grin and enthusiasm, she nodded enthusiastically. 'Oh, I'm sure. I'm looking forward to it immensely,' she replied, digging Tash in the ribs with her elbow to quell her giggles.

Looking momentarily perplexed at Tash's response, he rallied and carried on. 'How about you come to my office tomorrow morning? My door is always open as you know, but come around ten, and we can have some coffee and cake and a good ol' chat about your wonderful ideas!'

He stood next to them and pulled out his phone. 'Smile girls,' he called and snapped a couple of pictures. 'Another great shot for the feed!'

'Gosh, he's exhausting,' said Tash, as they watched him walk away, stopping and chatting to everyone that he walked past. 'He's the Ted Lasso of the skiing world!'

'Oh, he's sweet,' said Lola. 'Better than some bosses I've had.'

'I'll ask you again at the end of the season. Believe me, a couple of months of "Jolly Roger" will soon change your mind.'

Back in their cabin, as she snuggled up under the duvet in her room, Lola wondered what she was going to do about learning to ski. She knew Tash was going to be busy from now on. Her sister worked on the ski lifts and was up at the crack of dawn and usually exhausted by the time she got home.

As she drifted off, Luka's face swam into view, and she wondered how he had got that vicious scar that ran up his cheek. His startled look when she had exploded at him, literally, had been amusing, but he wasn't likely to want to help her now. Sighing to herself, she resolved to watch some more YouTube videos tomorrow. After all, how hard could it be?

Late the next afternoon, Lola arrived back at the cabin, threw her skis unceremoniously on the deck, banged the front door open and clumped inside. Pools of water collected at her feet as she yanked furiously to unzip her suit.

'Stupid, stupid, stupid snow. Stupid skiing and stupid me for thinking I could do this!' she exclaimed to the empty room as she yanked off the stupid boots. Pulling off her damp suit and leaving it where it fell, she walked to the kitchenette and poured herself a glass of milk and grabbed a packet of cookies from the overhead cupboard.

She had tried, she really had. Setting out with good intentions, her mind buzzing with all the information she had absorbed from the hours of videos she had studiously watched. It had been the most painful, humiliating, and mortifying life experience she'd had since middle school, when the school bully had grabbed her diary from her on the bus and exposed her immense crush on the art teacher to everyone who would listen.

But today had been so much worse. She had ended up chest deep in a snowdrift, having to be pulled out by three people. And that was before she even got up on the slope. Ignoring the dampness spreading through her cheap suit, she had struggled to the top of the kiddie slope and taken a deep breath to steady her nerves. Then she had promptly slid down it, sideways, emitting shrill screams all the way until she finally cartwheeled head over heels several times before landing in a bruised and crumpled heap, much to the amusement of the children following her down. Their laughter rang in her ears as she struggled to her feet, collected her skis that had flown off in opposite directions and trudged dejectedly home, pondering her reasons for being here.

When her sister came in from work a while later, she found Lola sitting dejectedly on the overstuffed armchair in front of the fire, her feet tucked up beneath her and a scattering of used tissues and biscuit crumbs around her. Her eyes were suspiciously red and the smile she gave strained.

'Things didn't go well, I take it?' she asked as she pulled off her coat and her boots. Lola just shook her head sadly.

'I just don't understand,' she moaned. 'I'm usually good at sports. Why can't I do this?'

'Probably because you hate snow,' her sister replied evenly, walking to the kitchenette and opening the bottle of wine on the counter. 'You like the beach, temperate climates, beach parties, snorkelling, and handball. Not four feet of snow and layers of clothing.'

'But I have to learn to ski to get through this season. I need to have completed a season in every resort type before I can apply for the manager's job in Cabo!'

'I know, hun, but we talked about this before you applied, and I told you we have to do the Christmas Extravaganza show *and* that you have to be able to ski. And to be honest, it's usually good fun. The kids are always so excited.'

'I get that. It's a lovely idea, I just don't think I can do it. Which means I will lose my job and this opportunity!'

'Well, Lola, you have two choices. You either give in and go home, *or* you talk to Luka and see if he can help you.'

Nodding slowly in reluctant agreement, Lola realised she was going to have to bite the bullet and try to talk that horrible man into helping her.

Chapter Four

Tilting his head at an angle so he could see better in the bathroom mirror, Luka carefully eased the razor up across the scarred surface of his face. The hairs around the puckered skin grew at random angles, and it was a test of patience every time he shaved. With a last check to make sure he had missed none, he flicked off the light and walked back into the main room of his cabin, grabbing his jumper off the back of the chair as he went.

Standing at the top of the steps of his porch, he was just zipping up his coat when he heard a tentative voice call out.

'Good morning.'

Reflexively flicking his scarf around his face, he looked up, amazed to see that woman standing there. The one who had crashed into him, and then spat wine on him. The one who, if he was completely honest, had been occupying his thoughts more than she should.

'Morning,' he responded, nodding curtly and walking down the stairs and past her, hoping she'd get the hint that he was a very busy man. *Apparently not*, he thought sourly, as she trotted along next to him, babbling away at him.

'I just wanted to apologise for spraying you with red wine the other night. Did you soak your shirt in vinegar? That's the best way to get it out, you know?'

Wincing at the thought of his poor shirt, abandoned in a crumpled heap on the floor of the bathroom along with the rest of that night's outfit, he muttered, 'I'm sure it will be fine. No need to apologise.'

Thinking that would be the end of it, it surprised him to find she continued to keep pace with him as he walked down the hill from the accommodation block into the village. After a moment's awkward silence, she blurted, 'I wanted to ask you about lessons.' He pulled up and looked at her, startled by the turn in conversation.

'I, ah... I only teach the little ones and beginners. You would need to check with the office to see if there is any availability for this week, though.'

'This week? I can do it any time,' she said, a cute frown wrinkling her forehead as she tilted her head at him.

Perplexed, Luka looked at her for a beat, before asking, 'how long are you on holiday for?'

She threw back her head and laughed. 'I'm so sorry,' she said, noticing the confusion on his face. 'I forgot, we haven't been formally introduced.' She stuck out her hand. 'I'm Lola, the new Events Coordinator for Loveland.'

Blindsided by this snippet of information, Luka automatically shook her hand. 'I see,' was all he could muster as his brain raced through the implications of the impression he must have made on her so far and, more importantly, the revenge she could take on him in her position. If she decided he should do a quick version of the Birdie dance, every day at lunchtime for the next few months, then he would have to comply. After Roger, the Events Coordinator held the baton of power, and they all had to bow to whatever hair-brained scheme they came up with.

'So, you can't ski?' he asked, surprised that any member of staff would be here without that basic skill. It was usually mandatory. Her face flushed, and her head dipped briefly before she brought her eyes back up to his and stared at him defiantly. 'Not particularly well,' she replied, blushing even further. 'That's why I thought you could help me.'

Disconcerted by the intensity of her gaze, Luka rallied his thoughts and tried to find a way out of this situation. He glanced at his watch. 'I have to go. My first class is waiting, but I will think about it.'

As he walked away, he could feel those intense brown eyes following him, and his insides squirmed a little. He should probably just have agreed to it straight away, but for some reason, the idea of spending time with Lola was firing up distress signals in his brain and the urge to get away was compelling.

The dilemma distracted him throughout the day, despite the constant demands of his junior classes. He coasted through the lessons on automatic pilot but, thankfully, his enthusiastic pupils didn't seem to notice. After his last lesson, he made his way thoughtfully back to his cabin, barely noticing the pain in his leg for a change. Instead of the usual steaming hot shower, he opened a bottle of wine and poured himself a glass.

Staring thoughtfully out of the window at the snowy village scene below him in the distance for a while, he finally came to the inevitable conclusion. Lola was going to be a big part of his life for the rest of the season, whether he liked it or not. So helping her with her request was the obvious choice, no matter how uncomfortable it made him. Throwing back the last of the wine for courage, he strode back out the door and down to the office block to find Lola before he could change his mind.

Chapter Five

'Hurry up, Lola,' Tash whined impatiently, twirling around in her chair, her ponytail flying out behind her. 'I told the guys we'd meet them in the bar.' Looking up from her spreadsheets, Lola smiled at her younger sister's petulant face. 'I won't be long. Why don't you go ahead without me? I'll catch up with you when I'm done.'

Tash stood up. 'Oh no, missy. I know you. If I leave, you will still be here in two hours' time, lost in the *fascinating* world of event planning and scheduling conflicts.'

Sighing, but closing her laptop anyway, Lola said, 'alright, alright. I just need to make sure that this year is the best year ever. I need to knock Roger's socks off to get that letter of recommendation.'

'Lola, every resort you have worked at for Sublime Retreats has given you a letter of recommendation. Why would Loveland be any different?'

'Because I can't ski, Tash! Plain and simple, and it doesn't look like that's going to change any time soon.'

'Well, I told you how to solve that. Speak to Luka, get him to teach you.'

'I did, this morning. He wasn't keen on the idea,' she replied dolefully, standing up and stretching out her aching back before starting to pack things away in her bag.

'Well, you should try... Hold that thought. Look who's here,' her sister chirped with a mischievous grin. Glancing up, Lola saw Luka striding down the hall towards her office with a look of determination. Ignoring the sudden skip of her heart, she forced a smile on her face, ready to greet him and be polite, whatever his decision.

'Luka, hi,' she said a little breathlessly. She coughed, then added more firmly, 'how can I help you?'

'Tomorrow. Meet me on the Green Slope at ten, and we'll see what we can do.'

'Umm... OK.' Lola squeaked. 'Can we... Can we do it earlier? I don't really want everyone gawping at me. Say, eight o'clock?' Luka nodded once, turned, and walked back up the hallway leaving both girls gaping after him.

'Well, there's a man of many words,' Tash giggled as she watched his retreating back. 'But at least he's agreed to help you.'

Lola felt heat rising to her face as she remembered telling him 'not particularly well' in response to his question about her skiing ability. Oh God, tomorrow he was going to see that, in fact, the term 'not at all' was actually the case. She snapped her bag shut. 'Come on, Tash, I need that drink now!'

The sisters pulled on their coats and, wrapped up in scarves and gloves, made their way out of the office block and down towards the village. The temperature was dropping, and they linked arms, huddled close as they wandered down the path.

'How's the big lighting-up event planning going?' asked Tash as they walked across the snow-covered village square towards the bar, the sound of muffled music becoming louder with each step. Dusk was falling and the chocolate-box-perfect wooden shops that surrounded the square were lit up with gaily twinkling lights to entice customers in.

'Oh, you know. It's getting there. I'm just waiting to hear back from some people. I really want to find someone big in the skiing world to come and do the switching on of the lights this year. Although I get the impression Roger won't be too keen.'

'I'm not surprised. He usually does it, and he plays Father Christmas in the Extravaganza. He loves being the centre of attention whenever possible.'

'I gathered that, but I'm hoping if I can get someone impressive enough, he will concede. After all, it will bring kudos to Loveland, which will reflect well on him. Maybe even get some news coverage.'

'What about Belinda McIntyre?'

'Who's she?'

'Good grief, Lola. Do you live in another world? She is only our most renowned ski jumper, and a model to boot. I happen to know Jolly Roger has a bit of a thing for her. I bet he wouldn't say no to her turning on his lights,' she said with a dirty chuckle.

'You are incorrigible!' Lola laughed, slapping her sister's arm. 'But that's a good idea, thanks.'

A blast of warmth, laughter, and music hit them as they pushed open the door to T-Bar, the favourite après-ski spot in the resort. Shedding their gloves, scarves, and coats as they went, they pushed their way through to the bar where Tash's friends were sitting. After Lola was introduced, with a flurry of names, to the lift crew her sister worked with, she settled on a stool and listened to their chatter, hoping to pick up some tips, as if by osmosis. But their banter did nothing to qualm her fears as they told comical stories which usually involved people face-planting in the snow. Their enthusiastic conversations about hitting the slopes at every possible chance were lost on Lola. She just couldn't see the attraction.

'Steve! Over here,' Tash suddenly called out. Glancing across, Lola saw her sister's face lit up like a Christmas tree. She turned on her stool to see who had caused this transformation and saw a tall, bearded man making his way through the crowd. He was obviously very popular, as he was stopped and greeted every other step. Especially by the women, Lola couldn't help but notice. When he finally reached them, Tash slipped off her stool and enveloped him in a hug. 'It's so good to see you! I thought you were working further north this year?'

'I was, but plans change,' he replied glibly, pulling back to grin at her. 'Wow. You're looking as fine as ever, Natasha. Makes me glad I came back.'

Lola's hackles rose, and she studied the man's face intently, but there was nothing but a big, crooked smile there. Maybe it was just her defensive big sister thing, she thought. As she glanced back at the bar, she noticed one of the group was also staring at Steve with something other than welcome. The guy who had been sitting next to her sister - she thought his name might have been Ben? Anyway, he looked less than thrilled to see Steve. *Interesting*, she thought, making a mental note to keep an eye on the situation as she watched Tash pull up a stool next to her for Steve.

The rest of the evening passed without incident until Lola finally made her excuses to leave. She was enjoying getting to know everyone; they were a fun crowd she was happy to find. Getting along with the various teams in the resort was a vital part of her role and also made the whole season easier. Living in enforced proximity with the people you worked with could be tough sometimes, as she well knew.

But the prospect of her first lesson with Luka tomorrow was weighing on her mind, and she was struggling to take part in the surrounding chatter, so she and Tash left the warmth of the bar to go home.

'Am I completely mad?' she asked her sister, who paused mid-brush of her teeth and stared back at her in the bathroom mirror. Taking a moment to rinse and spit, Tash replied. 'Mad for wanting your dream job? The job you've been coveting for years and the job that will mean you live just up the road from our grandparents? No, I don't think you're mad,' she laughed. 'A little *loca*, maybe. But you always go after what you want, Lola. I admire that about you. Don't worry, it will be worth it.'

'Thanks, Sis,' Lola said with a smile, which only faltered when she thought about Luka. 'I just hope you're right.'

Chapter Six

Luka stamped his boots impatiently as he waited for Lola the next morning. The air was heavy with the promise of more snow, and he was tired. He'd had a rough night, disturbed by the usual awful dreams, and was in no mood to be messed around. His plan was to get through this lesson as quickly as possible, tell her she was as good as she could be, and hopefully that would be enough. He spotted her; she was hard to miss in that ghastly pink suit, trudging across to him, skis awkwardly held in her arms, tripping her up with every other step.

'Hi Luka,' she puffed when she finally got to him, dropping the skis to the ground. 'Sorry I'm late. I was on a call and couldn't get away.'

'No problem,' he replied tersely without looking at her, annoyed that she thought his time was so easily dismissed. He pointed down the slope. 'OK, head down there and let me see what you can do.'

Lola carefully lined up her skis on the snow and tried to lock her boots onto them. The first one went in easily enough, but her other boot just refused to click into place. After a few seconds of watching her helpless attempts, Luka knelt down, grumbling under his breath. Brushing away the lump of snow that had collected on the bottom of her boot, he grabbed her calf firmly and pulled her foot into position, roughly forcing it down.

'Ow,' she cried as she lost her balance and clung to his shoulders for support. 'No need to be so violent!'

He looked up at her, and once again found himself mesmerised by her large, brown eyes. Shaking himself away from her gaze and her touch, he stood up and said gruffly, 'I don't have all day.'

He watched as she stared down the slope. Her face was white and pinched as she took in deep breaths, slowly blowing out through pursed lips. She glanced at him and burst out with, 'so, how long have you been working here?'

Puzzled, he responded, 'three years. Now go down the slope.'

'But do you like it? I mean, working here, with the kids and everything?'

'Yes, it's fine. Now go down the slope.'

'I wanted to ask where you're from,' she rushed. 'I mean the accent. Obviously not local,' she finished with a forced grin.

'I am from Quebec,' he replied smoothly, rubbing his scarred cheek with his knuckles. 'Now go down the slope.'

She stared off into the distance for a beat, before admitting in a small voice, 'I don't want to.'

'*Calice de Crisse!* What is wrong with you? You force me to come out here in my free time, and now you say you "don't want to." Are you completely mad? You are worse than the children.'

Lola's face flushed, and she glared at him. 'Fine. I'm going!'

With another deep breath, she pushed off and sailed down the slope at a bizarre angle, with all the grace of Bambi taking his first steps. She didn't get very far before her skies crossed over, and she fell awkwardly with a tiny yelp that sparked something in him, and he ran to where she lay, ignoring the pain that shot up his leg.

'Are you alright?' he asked, looking worriedly down at her. Lola's eyes were closed; she looked defeated somehow. But after a moment, her usual defiant expression reappeared as her eyes flashed back open and she glared up at him.

'I can't ski, OK? I have never skied, never wanted to ski, and I still don't want to. But I have to be able to for this job!' Her chest was heaving up and down at the end of this rant, and he found himself momentarily distracted before her words sank in.

'How on earth did you get a job here if you can't ski?'

'Well, they never actually asked,' she said, pushing herself up and reclaiming her poles, which had flown off to one side when she fell. 'I think they just kinda assumed, you know. Because I applied and, well, my sister works here. I guess they thought if she can do it, I can too.'

Despite himself, he started to laugh. He tried to hold it back, but she looked so ridiculous and fractious he couldn't help himself, and it exploded out of him. A flash of anger crossed her face, but only briefly before she grinned back at him and started giggling. 'It is kind of a dumb situation, isn't it?' she chuckled and held out her hand. He took it and helped her back to her feet.

'You could say that. Mon Dieu, what possessed you to apply? Is it something you wanted to learn? Did you think you could just wing it?' She was looking up at him through her dark lashes, her eyes shining with amusement, but he noticed a flicker of concern flare through them.

'Honestly? It is the last thing I want to do, and yes, I thought I could wing it. I'm usually good at sporty things,' she said, unclipping her skis and stepping towards him. 'But you see, I have to learn. I know there is a position coming up for next summer at Sublime Retreats' Cabo resort, and I really, really want that job.'

Taken aback by her closeness, he stumbled back and mumbled, 'so why Loveland?'

'The job in Cabo is for a resort manager. I have worked in every type of resort they have so far, European Villas, City Breaks, you name it. All of them except a ski resort, so I picked the one where my sister works. I need to have done my time in all of them...'

'To get the job,' he finished for her, finally understanding.

'Exactly. So please, please help me,' she said quietly, stepping into his space yet again, looking up into his eyes. He gulped, aware of the faint scent of jasmine, and moved another step back.

'Is... is this job in Cabo so important?'

'Yes, it is. I want to be near my grandparents. They are very important to me, and this is the best way I can be close to them.'

Taken aback by her honesty and the pleading look in her eyes, he nodded once.

'*D'accord.* Then let us start again.'

Chapter Seven

An hour later, Lola was battered and bruised. The muscles in her legs were aching in bizarre places, and she was frozen to the bone. Looking up at Luka from her current sprawled out position in the snow, she asked, 'can we take a break? I'm not sure how much more humiliation I can take today.'

He smiled down at her as he replied. 'Sure. I think you have had enough for today, and I have to get ready for my next class.' She stared up at him, admiring the curve of his jaw and the way his blue eyes crinkled at the edges when he smiled.

'What? What are you staring at?' he demanded, shifting uncomfortably under her gaze.

'You,' she replied simply. 'Your face completely changes when you smile. You should do it more often,' she added with a grin, still savouring his face. 'Are you blushing? You are!' she laughed, spreading out her arms and legs like a starfish and waving them back and forth.

'What on earth are you doing?'

'I'm making a snow angel. It's fun, you should try it.'

'I don't think so,' he said tersely. 'Come on, Lola, stop mucking around.'

Grumbling that he was no fun, she stood up, brushing the clumps of snow off her legs.

'So, how do you think I'm doing?' she asked as they made their way off the slope, down the path that led into the village and beyond to their accommodation. He gave a snort. 'I think we have a long way to go. You spent more time on the ground than skiing.'

His words stung, but she knew he was right, and her mind skipped off to the unhappy place where thoughts of losing her job and what it would mean overwhelmed her and her shoulders sagged dejectedly.

'Hey,' he said, placing a hand on her arm to stop her. 'Tell me, why is this so important? I mean, I care about my grandparents, but…' he trailed off.

Lola stared off into the middle distance for a moment before slowly answering. 'They brought me up. Well, us up. Tash and me, after our parents died,' she breathed, not able to look directly at him. His hand dropped away with a sharp intake of breath.

'God, I'm sorry,' he said, sounding contrite, and she gave him a small smile.

'It's not your fault, don't be sorry,' she said glibly, her stock answer to this inevitable statement. 'It happened a long time ago.'

'Of course it's not my fault, but I can still be sorry,' he said seriously, pulling her around so he could look directly at her. 'Let us try again tomorrow morning. Same time, same place?' He was smiling gently at her. Lola realised there was more to this man than the gruff exterior he presented to the world, and was alarmed to note that she would quite like to find out what else hid beneath that prickly surface.

'That would be great, thanks,' she said brusquely, pushing that idea away. 'Anyway, I'd better get off. Things to organise, people to see!' She hurried off back to her cabin, her mind whirling with frantic thoughts. She needed to focus on learning to ski and making it through this season successfully, not getting distracted by attractive ski instructors and the possibilities hinted at by those amazing blue eyes that made her heart beat so swiftly.

After she had showered and changed into her favourite jeans and a warm jumper, she made her way to the office block, stopping off at the bakery in the village along the way and trying to keep her mind on the plan that she had for the Lighting up Loveland ceremony. She had spoken with the agent for Belinda McIntyre this morning, and he had seemed quite keen on her request. Lola couldn't wait to see if he had emailed to let her know the star's response and prayed it would be positive.

The offices were made up of prefab buildings, clad with wooden panels to look authentic and severely lacking in insulation. She was standing in the kitchen warming her hands and blowing on her mug of coffee, lost in thought, when Tash came bustling past. She paused at the door when she caught sight of Lola.

'Hey, Sis, how'd it go with Mr Grumpy?'

Lola laughed cheerlessly. 'Not so great, I'm afraid.'

'I hope he wasn't too mean to you. I'll be pissed if he upsets you!'

'No, no. Actually, he was fine. I meant me, not so great, you know, the staying upright thing.'

'Ah, well, OK.' her sister smiled back at her, and walked in to give her a hug. 'Don't worry, you'll get there, eventually. And hopefully before we have to do the Extravaganza!'

'Let's hope so. Anyway, what are you doing here?'

Her sister's gaze skittered off as she replied, 'oh, I just had to catch hold of Roger. There was some mix-up with the schedules for the lift crew that I needed to sort out.'

'Hmm, and did you happen to stop off at the hire shop where a certain hunky person works?'

Tash had the decency to look embarrassed, but she laughed and put up her hands. 'You caught me.' she said. 'But I really did need to see Roger. Anyway, shall we catch up at the T-Bar later? About six?'

'Sure, that would be good,' Lola told her, pushing away from the counter and walking towards her office. 'Stay out of trouble,' she called back over her shoulder, causing Tash to grin impishly as she left.

As she scanned through her emails, Lola was delighted to see a reply from the agent in her inbox and hastily scanned through it, a wide smile breaking out as she read that Belinda was, indeed, interested in coming to Loveland. She was going to have to talk to Roger about the idea now, and see if he was as enamoured of the star as Tash thought he was.

Grabbing the bag of doughnuts she had bought for this purpose, she made her way down the hall and rapped on the open door of his office to alert him of her presence.

'Lola!' he beamed, standing up. 'How lucky am I? I get to see both the Sanchez sisters this morning. Come in, come in,' he said, gesturing to the chair in front of his desk. 'What can I do for you on this fine morning?'

'Well, first I wanted to give these to you,' she said, placing the bag on the desk, happy to see his eyes light up as he opened it.

'That's very thoughtful of you,' he said through his first mouthful of the sugary confection, scattering crumbs on the paperwork in front of him, then wiping his mouth with the back of one hand. 'You said first, so I assume there's a second?' he chuckled, taking another bite.

'Um, yes, there is. I wanted to talk to you about the Lighting up Loveland ceremony coming up.'

His chewing paused for a moment, and he washed it down with a mouthful of coffee.

'My favourite event,' he said cautiously, his usual smile disappearing into a frown. 'What about it?'

'I was thinking that we could get someone else to turn on the lights this year. You know, someone famous?'

'Lola, Lola,' he said with an avuncular tone, standing and turning to look out of the window, hands clasped behind his back. 'I have been turning on the lights here for the last decade. Our guests expect me to do it. *They* all look forward to it.'

'I realise that, but I thought maybe getting someone well known in the skiing world would add more pizazz to the process. You know, make a real event of it, possibly get some newspaper coverage?'

He stilled, and she knew she had caught his attention, so she rushed on to close the deal. 'Anyway, Belinda McIntyre has said she would love to come and turn on the lights. But if you don't think it's a good idea, I completely understand.'

He spun around to look at her, his face shiny and red, eyes alight with excitement. Lola had to hold in a giggle as she stood. 'It was a silly idea, sorry. I'll email her now and say that you will turn on the lights as usual.'

'Now hold on, hold on,' he blustered. 'Let me think about this for a minute,' he plopped back into his chair. 'Maybe there is something in your idea.'

Taking his cue, she sat back down and watched the internal struggle play out across his features as he tried to figure out how to save face and get to meet the woman of his dreams at the same time.

'You know, I had been toying with the thought of doing something different this year.'

'Really?' Lola asked, big eyed, still playing along. 'So, do you think this could work?'

'You know it just might, it just might. And it would be great for our Instagram feed,' he said dreamily. His eyes snapped back into focus. 'Belinda definitely said she would do it?'

'Oh yes, she seemed quite keen. I just need to hash out the details of her fee and accommodation, things like that.'

'Hmm,' he uttered, pretending to look thoughtful. 'Well, let's run with this idea of yours for now. I mean, you never know until you try, do you?' he finished, finally allowing the smile of joy and excitement to brighten his face.

Grinning back at him, she stood up again and managed to say with a straight face, 'thank you Roger. I really appreciate you allowing me to try something different. Not all managers would be so trusting.'

She didn't think his smile could stretch any further, but it did. 'Well, Lola. I like to think of myself as approachable and hands-on, you know that.'

Nodding in agreement, she took her leave, finally allowing the giggles to erupt when she was back in the safety of her office.

Chapter Eight

Nursing his drink in the T-Bar, Luka sat, oblivious to the surrounding jocularity, lost in a world of reminiscence and regret. As a rule, he tried not to dwell on the accident that had changed the course of his life forever. But some days, like today, when his leg ached despite the painkillers and his life seemed pointless, it overwhelmed him.

A blast of icy air hit him as the door of the bar swung open again, and he glanced up and saw Lola unwrapping the scarf from her neck, scanning the bar, looking for someone. Her eyes finally landed on him and her face lit up in a way that caused his insides to twist alarmingly.

'Hey,' she said, coming over to him. 'Can I sit here for a while? I'm supposed to be meeting my sister, but time-keeping is not her strong suit.' She plonked herself down on the wooden chair opposite him without waiting for a response. 'How was the rest of your day?'

'As you would expect,' he said sourly, his expression darkening further as he took a sip of his beer.

She cocked her head and contemplated him across the table. 'Why do I always get the impression you don't like it here?'

'I have nothing against this place,' he replied, standing up. 'Can I get you a drink?' he asked quickly, before she could probe further. She pointed at his beer.

'One of those would be great, thanks.'

Pushing his way to the bar, Luka tried to rein in his morbid thoughts and replace the scowl on his face with something more amenable. He knew people thought he was miserable and unapproachable, and if he was honest, he cultivated that image. It was all part of his denial of what his life had become. He didn't want to fit in; he didn't belong here, and keeping people at arm's length suited him. At the bar, he ordered a round, and while he waited, he realised that Lola seemed unaffected by his demeanour. She was like a puppy that kept coming back, no matter how much you shooed it away. At that thought, he grinned despite himself, and by the time he returned to the table, he could give her a genuine smile.

'Here you go,' he said, sliding a bottle across the table to her and taking his seat.

'Thanks, I need this,' she said fervently. 'I'm still recovering from my lesson this morning,' she laughed, draining a couple of mouthfuls. 'And I still want to know why you don't like it here.'

Luka sighed; he should have known she wouldn't give up her line of questioning. Returning her steady gaze for a moment, he considered his options. He never spoke about his accident or the life he had before it had happened, but he had the feeling that this woman would not take his usual non-committal responses for an answer. He also remembered her sharing a little of her life with him earlier, something else he was sure that didn't get talked about much.

'It's not that I don't like it here,' he replied eventually. 'I should just be somewhere else.'

Lola was still staring at him expectantly, so he continued. 'I was a ski jumper. Quite a good one. I was set to take part in the Winter Olympics but then this...' his hand flapped vaguely at his left side.

'This what? The scar? You had an accident?' she asked, leaning forward, elbows resting on the table, completely, disconcertingly, focused on him.

'You ask a lot of questions, don't you?'

'And you are avoiding them,' she replied smartly.

He chuckled. 'Yes, I am. I don't like to talk about it. But, to satisfy your curiosity and end this line of questioning, yes, I had an accident. But the damage is much greater than is visible on my face. I shattered my leg into many pieces. They bolted it together as best they could, but bye-bye Olympics and everything else that was important to me. So, now I am here, teaching kids to ski.'

'That's not such a terrible place to be,' she said, smiling at him gently.

'Perhaps.'

She gazed at him for a long minute before saying, 'in my experience, you have to let go of what has gone before. Especially the things that are out of your control and you can't change.'

'Easier said than done,' he bit back. 'But anyway, enough of this. How are your plans to entertain our guests going?'

Lola desperately wanted to keep that conversation going and find out more, but she could see the discomfort etched on his face, so she nodded slightly instead and replied.

'Quite well, actually. I've convinced Roger to let someone else turn on the lights this year!'

A bark of laughter escaped him. 'Good God. How on earth did you manage that?'

'A generous mix of sugar and an idol,' she replied enigmatically, grinning happily at him.

Before he could investigate that statement further, her phone chimed. Lola picked it up and read the message, her face falling into a frown.

'What's up?' he asked.

'My little sister, that's what,' she replied angrily, throwing the phone back on the table. 'She's cancelled on me. I guess she had a more interesting offer, and I also guess that offer was called Steve.'

It took a moment for Luka to place the name. When he did, all sorts of rumours came to mind regarding the man in question. He wasn't one to gossip, but he also wanted to warn Lola, so he struggled to find a way to let her know Steve was bad news.

'She should be careful with that one,' was the best he could come up with.

'Why? What's wrong with him?' she demanded.

'Let's just say he's a bit of a ladies' man,' he said guardedly, not wanting to repeat all that he had heard.

Lola gave a dramatic sigh and sank back in her chair. 'Why am I not surprised?' she said, draining her beer. 'Tash always seems to find them.' She looked lost in thought for a minute before standing up decisively. 'I better head back to my cabin.'

'Are you sure you wouldn't like another?' Luka asked, amazed to find he wanted to keep talking with her. But she shook her head as she smiled down at him.

'No, I want to have a clear head so I can have a *chat* with Tash when she gets back. But I'll see you in the morning?'

'I shall look forward to it.'

'I'm glad one of us will,' she muttered, but grinned at him before she left, leaving his heart fluttering strangely and feeling happier than before.

Chapter Nine

Back in her cabin, Lola changed into her pyjamas and curled up on the couch near the fire with a book to read as she settled in to wait for Tash, but she couldn't concentrate. Her mind kept drifting back to the conversation with Luka, and how it made her feel when he smiled at her.

Not wanting to dwell on it too deeply, she pushed the blanket off her legs and stood to go to the kitchenette and make some hot chocolate. The only advantage, in her opinion, of being stuck in a ski resort was it gave her a darn fine excuse to treat herself to her favourite drink whenever she fancied.

A noise outside the front door alerted her to her sister's return. After a moment, when the door didn't open, she went to the window and pushed the curtain aside to look and saw Tash, wrapped in the arms of the tall, bearded man who she distrusted immensely. Stepping back so they didn't see her, she scurried and took up her position on the sofa again, pulling the blanket back over her legs.

'Oh, hi,' she said nonchalantly when the door finally

opened, revealing her sister with a love-struck look on her face. 'How was your evening? I assume, by the soppy look on your face, you were with Steve?' Lola tried to keep her tone neutral, but Natasha knew her far too well to be fooled.

'I take it you're not too keen on him,' she said huffily, as she unzipped her coat and hung it on the rack next to the door before bending to unlace her boots.

'I don't know the man,' Lola said evenly, still trying to cover what she was thinking.

'Exactly!' Tash responded. 'So don't go forming opinions on people you don't know. Just because you don't think any man is good enough for you, that doesn't mean I have to live by your ridiculous standards.' Tash stomped over to the sink and ran the tap for a glass of water, pointedly keeping her back to Lola.

With a sigh, Lola stood. The last thing she wanted was to fall out with her sister over this. She was fairly sure this so-called relationship wasn't going anywhere, and she was determined not to let this man put a wedge between them. Walking over to where Tash stood, she wrapped her arms around her rigid form and lay her head on her back.

'I just like to look out for you, you know? You're my Lil Sis,' she said, using her childhood nickname. Tash let out a breath and relaxed into her embrace.

'I know, I know. But sometimes you can be too overprotective.'

'Well, I've had to look out for you for so long. Ever since...' she paused, not wanting to complete the sentence. Tears stung her eyes as she relived that dreadful day when they were plucked out of school by two police officers. She could still remember the look on her headmistress's face when she came to class and told her she had to go with them. That look of pity had stayed with her ever since. She was nine at the time, Tash three years younger, and since that moment she had felt bound by the responsibility of looking after her sister.

Tash spun around and hugged her fiercely, not needing to say anything. The sisters clung to each other, united in their grief and loss, all thoughts of the disagreement pushed away for now. They pulled apart with watery smiles.

'Just promise to give him a chance,' Tash said with a sniff and a grin. Lola considered her for a moment before nodding. 'Fair enough, I will,' she said, ignoring her instincts screaming to warn her sister of this man. 'But I don't appreciate being stood up.' She gave her shoulder a playful push. 'Next time we have an arrangement, keep it!'

'I'm sorry. I know I shouldn't have done that. In the future, I promise not to leave you stranded by yourself. I hope you weren't too uncomfortable.'

'Actually, it was fine. Luka was there, so I sat with him for a while.'

Tash smirked. 'Oh, yes? Is there something going on between you two that I should know about?'

Turning away on the pretext of collecting her cup from the table to hide the heat that had blossomed on her face, she called over her shoulder, 'don't be silly. He was just there, and you weren't!'

'Hmm,' Tash said, but obviously let it slide. 'Well, I'm off to bed. I'm on the early shift tomorrow, so I need my beauty sleep. Night, Sis.'

'Goodnight, Tash, sleep tight.'

Lola cleaned her cup and left it to drain beside the sink before following Tash through to the bathroom to brush her teeth. In bed, she stared at the ceiling, unable to get her concerns about her sister's choice in men and worries about losing her job out of her head. She huffed and turned on her side, trying to get comfortable. She had an early start, too. She had to meet the broody Luka at eight for her next lesson. A little thrill ran through her at the thought, and she chided herself for being as feckless as her sister. But as she drifted off, it was his blue eyes and his smile she was thinking of.

Chapter Ten

The next morning, Luka was so exhausted he could barely see straight. Another night of sparse sleep and vivid dreams when he did manage to drift off left him restless and irritable. The only thing that got him moving was the knowledge that he would see Lola this morning. It was misty and damp outside, low clouds being swirled through the trees by the strong breeze, and the ache in his leg started before he even made it to the slope. He considered returning home to take his painkillers, but he didn't want to be late for Lola.

Aggrieved when he arrived that there was no sign of her, he paced up and down to ease the ache in his leg and keep his mind from spiralling. Finally, he spotted the fluorescent glow of her suit bobbing up the hill. He smiled at her gawkiness as she stumbled up to him, carrying her equipment.

'Morning, Luka,' she huffed when she got to him, dropping everything on the ground in a heap.

'Bonjour, how are you today?' he asked, desperate to

move the fronds of hair that were sticking to her forehead, but keeping his hands firmly in his pockets.

She looked bleakly down the slope. 'Alright, I guess. I'm just not looking forward to this.'

Disappointment shot through him; she obviously wasn't as pleased to see him as he was to see her.

'Well, we can always cancel,' he snapped, turning away. Lola glanced up at him, alarmed.

'No, no! I didn't mean that. Sorry, I'm being a defeatist. Just getting up here seems like such hard work,' she sighed. 'It feels like I will never get the hang of this.'

He laughed and placed a consoling hand on her shoulder. 'Lola, you have only had one lesson. Give me a chance. I'm good, but not that good. I can't magically make you ski in one hour!'

She smiled at him sheepishly, her eyes lighting up with amusement. 'I guess I am a little impatient.'

'Just a bit,' he grinned, rubbing her shoulder, then stepping away. Hiding his feelings behind his professional face he said, 'Ok, I think today, the first lesson is how to walk.'

She looked at him with an expression that was a comical mix of confusion and offence. 'I have been able to walk by myself for quite a few years now.'

'Ah, yes. But walking in ski boots is an entirely different thing. Look.' He turned and walked up the slope a little to show her. 'Walking up a hill you need to go toe first, kicking into the snow, like this.' He stopped and looked back at her. 'Now you try.'

Frowning in concentration, she followed him up, the first few steps faltering, and then she got it, delight blooming on her face. 'God, that's much easier,' she beamed at him. 'It's still not comfortable in these boots, though. I hate the way you can't move your ankle. It feels weird.'

Ignoring the spark of happiness at her delight and her complaints about the boots, he continued. 'So, now we have to go down, we use the heel. Watch.' He walked back down, firmly wedging his heels into the ground with each step. Lola nodded and copied his movement, following him down. At the last step, her boot shot out in front of her and she thumped onto her back, her boot catching his left leg.

Excruciating pain flamed through his leg and he stifled a cry and the angry retort that flew to his lips.

'Oh my God, I'm so sorry,' she cried, scrambling to her feet in front of him. Luka bent his head, taking deep breaths to ride out the pain. After a moment, it subsided a little, and he looked up. She was inches away from him, concern blazing from those beautiful eyes. His stomach lurched, and he stumbled back before he could give in to the overwhelming urge to kiss her.

'It's nothing,' he growled. 'Now, try that again. This time, try to stay upright!'

Looking chastised, Lola did as she was told, and after several attempts at going up and down, she became more confident in her steps, adding a little jump to each one and grinning like a child.

'What's next, boss?' she called gaily. 'Shall I put on my skis?'

'Non. Now you are going to learn how to carry them, so it doesn't take you half an hour to get here and make you late every time.'

Her face fell, but she nodded meekly and watched his instruction with fierce concentration. She quickly seized the concept of locking the skis together, carrying them jauntily over her shoulder as she marched around.

'I feel like a real skier now,' she claimed jubilantly.

'You have a long way to go,' he replied tersely, not

daring to look in her direction. He then showed her how to scuff her boots on the toe piece of the binding to remove any snow before clicking them into the skis. All the while, he was refusing to look at her, battling against his growing attraction to her. His leg was still throbbing from the earlier blow, and he was getting grumpier by the second.

'Now can I try going down?' she asked hopefully.

'Nope. I want you to put on one ski, and you are going to slide along, across this flat section. Use your poles and your other boot to push yourself along. Let's see if you can do that.'

A flash of anger flew across her face. She was biting her lower lip and he could tell she was holding back a comment. The wind had picked up and was whipping her hair about her face. That and her terse expression reminded him of medusa.

'Look, I should have started with all this last time,' he said, trying to make his tone less harsh.

'Well, why didn't you?' She said crossly, glaring at him.

'I didn't realise how incompetent you were,' he snapped back. 'Now, if you want to learn to ski, please do as I say.'

Without a word, she did as she was told, but he could see that any enthusiasm she'd had for the lesson had long gone. After she had made a few passes, he called a halt to the lesson.

'I think that's enough for today.'

Lola looked at him in shock. 'What do you mean? I haven't done anything yet.'

'You have learnt the basics, which is a good start. And I have other things to do.'

She remained sullenly silent as they made their way off the slope, only speaking as they walked under the ski lifts. She looked up and watched as they crossed overhead, the hum of the wires interrupted at intervals by the creak of the cars as they shifted in the wind.

'Bet that's a bit bumpy today.'

Looking up instinctively, Luka flinched as dread flickered through him like a dark cloud.

'I have to go,' he mumbled and sped off as fast as his aching leg would allow, across the snow, leaving Lola wondering what the hell was wrong with him.

Chapter Eleven

Lola was disgruntled as she went home to get changed for work. She felt as if she had achieved nothing in this morning's lesson and she would never be able to ski. Luka's grumpy attitude didn't help. He was so annoying. Good cop and bad cop all rolled up into one infuriating package. She would never understand what made him tick.

As she walked through the village, her mood lifted. There was a festive air about the place now. The ground team was putting up the Christmas decorations and lights, and despite the dismal weather, everyone had smiles on their faces. She followed the path down to where the ice-skating rink was being set up. Tonight was the grand opening, and she wanted to make sure everything was on schedule before starting her day.

Content that all was as it should be, she made her way to the office building. There was a whole host of activities and events lined up for the upcoming weeks, and it soon distracted her from her skiing worries as she worked her way through the plans. Checking things off and highlighting the items she still needed to take action on held her attention.

A rap on her door brought her out of her scheduling trance and she looked up to see Gayle, the head of the children's entertainment team, smiling at her.

'Hi, am I disturbing you?'

Pushing her hair behind her ears, Lola stood and returned her smile. 'Not at all, Gayle. Please, come in.' She liked Gayle. The woman was around her age and, from what she had seen so far, very competent at her job.

'What can I do for you?'

'I just wanted to talk to you about these extra activity ideas that you sent through,' Gayle replied, waving a printout of the email Lola had sent yesterday.

'Don't you like the ideas?' Lola asked, worried that she'd missed the mark.

'No, it's not that. They're great,' she said with a reassuring smile. 'It's just that I don't have enough staff to cover all of these, along with their regular duties.'

Lola frowned, nodding slowly. 'That is an issue. I'm not sure we have the funding to employ extra staff at this stage,' she said thoughtfully. 'What if I can find a way to rota in some help from the rest of the team?'

'I'm sure they'll be none too happy about it, but that would be a big help, yes,' she replied with a grin.

'Let me have a word with Roger and see what we can do,' Lola said, standing. 'The extra activities are only an hour or so. I'm certain there is a way they can take back that time at another part of the day or later in the season.'

'Great, thanks. Keep me posted.'

Lola followed her out of the door and went to find Roger. She found him in his office and he greeted her with his usual sunny smile as she walked in and took her seat.

'Can I run something past you?' she asked once the niceties were over.

A look of panic crossed his face. 'Is everything OK with the lighting ceremony? She's still coming, isn't she?' he asked pleadingly.

'Yes, yes, that's all fine,' she reassured him and he settled back and listened to her proposal.

'Hm,' he said, steepling his fingers in front of his face. 'Now, there's a sticky conundrum. Sticky indeed.'

'I was thinking, as it is only these few activities leading up to Christmas, we can give them an extra half day later in the season when things are quieter, to make up for it?'

'That might do the trick! There will still be some grumbling, but at the end of the day we are one team and we all need to do what we can, hey?'

'Exactly, and just think of the Instagram posts with the staff having fun with the kids. Decorating cookies, making snowmen? It will be great publicity.'

He beamed at her. 'I have to say, you really are a top-notch organiser. You have a real flair for maximising our exposure. Top-notch indeed.'

At the end of the day Lola returned to her cabin, tired but satisfied with how the rest of her day had worked out. Tash was there, morosely flicking through channels on the TV.

'Hey, Sis,' she called as Lola came in. 'How did your lesson go?'

Lola dumped her bag on a chair and took off her coat, pulling a face. 'Pretty dreadful. That man is a pain in the you know what!'

'We knew that,' Tash laughed. 'What's he done now?'

Lola explained the events of the morning, getting irate all over again.

'To be fair, it sounds like he did the right thing. I mean, you have to learn to walk before you can ski,' Tash said in a mollifying tone, giggling at her own joke.

'Hilarious,' Lola scowled at her. 'At least the rest of the day went well. The ice skating rink opens tonight and I have a few other things lined up for the kids.'

Tash sat up. 'Ice skating? I'd forgotten that it was today. We should go.'

'Whatever for? I doubt my skills in that department are any better than on the slopes,' Lola replied fractiously, plopping down onto the couch next to her sister.

'Come on, it will be fun,' Tash exclaimed excitedly. 'And it could help. If you get the hang of skating, it totally helps when you ski.'

'Really?' Lola arched a disbelieving eyebrow at her sister.

'Yes, really, it's true and vice versa. Google it if you don't believe me!'

'What about Steve? Aren't you seeing him tonight?'

Tash looked downcast for a moment. 'He said he was busy. Which leaves me at a loose end. Come on, Sis, please.'

Defeated, Lola gave in. 'OK, let me have a shower and get ready and we'll go and check it out. I'm not promising to put on the boots, though.'

Laughing, Tash jumped up. 'We'll see!'

Wrapped up warmly, the sisters joined the stream of people making their way out of the main square of the village towards the new rink.

'Looks like this idea of yours is proving popular,' Tash told her with a grin, which Lola returned happily. The pop-up rink was one of the few of her ideas that she hadn't had to cajole Roger into. He had happy childhood memories of skating, it seemed, and immediately agreed it was a fine idea. Sure enough, when they arrived, he was already on the ice, showing off his moves.

The girls watched him strut his stuff with amusement as he gyrated and spun to the disco beat that was pulsing across the rink. When he spotted them, he glided over, grasping the barrier in front of them, panting.

'Hey girls, get your skates on. This is great fun!'

'I'm game,' Tash said instantly, casting a sly look at her sister.

'I'm not sure, Roger,' Lola stammered. 'I've never skated before.'

'Poppycock! If you can ski, you can skate,' he declared happily. 'I'll see you out there.' With that, he pushed off and joined the turning tide of people gliding around the rink.

'I'll get you back for this,' she muttered to her sister as she pulled her along to the counter to find some boots.

Chapter Twelve

Luka had arranged to meet Ben at the T-Bar after work. He'd known him since his first year working at Loveland, and he was the closest thing he had to a friend on the resort. Ben was an affable young man who seemed to take not a blind bit of notice of his erratic moods and occasional outbursts, and Luka found he could relax in his company.

Ben leapt off his stool and embraced him in a one-arm manly hug when he arrived, slapping him vigorously on the back with the other hand.

'Good to see you, Luka. Beer?' he asked with a grin on his boyish face.

Luka nodded and hoisted himself onto the stool next to him. 'How's work going?' he asked while they waited to be served.

'Oh, the usual. Although it was pretty windy today. I thought we might have to close the lifts at one point, but it was OK in the end.'

Luka stiffened, not saying a word, and grabbed the beer

when it arrived on the bar in front of them. He took a swift gulp, then looked around, noticing the lack of customers.

'It's pretty quiet in here tonight.'

'Yeah, I think most people have gone to the opening of the ski rink that Lola's set up,' Ben told him, glancing around at the mostly empty bar. The door swung open and Steve sauntered in, ushering a young girl before him. Frowning over his beer, Ben watched them with hooded eyes, his face impassive.

'I wonder where Tash is,' he mused quietly, as he watched them sit close together at a table in the corner.

'Probably with her sister at that skating nonsense,' Luka retorted, not wanting to think about Lola and the mess of emotions that she brought up. He felt bad for the way he had treated her during their lesson today, but he needed to keep his defences up and maintain his distance.

Ben sat up, a keen look on his face. 'Maybe we should swing by and see how it's going?'

'I don't think so,' he replied darkly, taking another swig of beer. Although it would be nice to see Lola. It might even give him a chance to be a little nicer to her. She might appreciate his support at this new endeavour, if nothing else.

Ben nudged his shoulder. 'Come on. It's gotta be better than watching that idiot fawning over his latest conquest. And I know you can skate. You told me you used to play hockey?'

'This is true,' Luka grumbled, partially swayed but wondering if seeing her again would make the situation better or worse. Ben glanced at his phone and chuckled. 'Look,' he grinned, holding it up so he could see the screen. 'Roger is already there doing his best disco moves!'

Shaking his head in amusement, Luka took the phone

and stared at the post. Roger beaming at the camera, face dappled by disco lights. #lovelandrocks

'Ok, let's go see him in action,' he agreed, all at once keen to get there and see Lola. They paid their tab, and with a last disdainful look at Steve, made their way out into the night. The area around the rink was buzzing with activity. Crowds of people watched on, and Luka scanned the faces, trying to find Lola in the throng as they walked through. Surprised that he couldn't see her - after all this was her grand idea - he followed Ben to the counter to get some ice skates.

He had to shout his size over the music to the girl behind the counter and once he had his boots, turned towards the rink and its pulsing rope lights to see where the benches were. Ben pointed them out, and they used them to change into the skates. Looking up from lacing the second one, he finally spotted Lola clinging to the edge of the barrier on the other side of the rink. He watched her for a moment and his heart swelled at her hopeless attempts to move. Not waiting for Ben, he went onto the ice and followed the crowd around until he reached her.

'I see you skate as well as you ski,' he said into her ear. She was facing away from him and jumped in shock at his voice, feet wildly skidding as she tried to keep her balance. 'What are you doing here?' she demanded truculently, her face screwed up in displeasure. Ignoring her expression, he gently pulled her reluctant hands from the barrier and turned her to face him.

'Don't look at your feet,' he instructed firmly. 'Just look at my eyes.' He slowly started to skate backwards, pulling her with him. Her skates slid out from under her, and she stumbled, but he held her firm. 'I said just look at my eyes!'

She obeyed and locked eyes with him. His heart stuttered, but he kept going, gently leading her around the rink. Her hands grasped his forearms a little tighter every time she slipped, but her eyes remained focused on him. Her frown of concentration made him smile, she looked so cute and determined he nearly lost balance himself.

'What are you grinning at?' she said crossly. 'I don't know why you always find my predicaments so amusing.'

'I'm admiring your tenacity,' he replied, tilting his head towards the rest of the rink. 'I'm guessing this is the last thing you want to be doing right now, but here you are.'

She finally allowed him a smile. 'Never let it be said that Lola Sanchez didn't rise to a challenge.'

'I wouldn't dream of it,' he grinned, speeding up. Her mouth opened into an Oh of surprise, but she kept pace with her usual fiery determination. After a couple of revolutions of the rink, he pulled her up as they reached the exit.

'Need a break?'

She was panting with exertion but looked like she was going to refuse out of sheer pigheadedness, so he jumped in. 'I could use one. Shall we get a drink?'

'Sure, if *you* need one,' she said and stumbled out of the rink, flopping gratefully onto a bench. Still grinning, he followed and offered to go to the bar. When he got back with their drinks, she had regained her composure and was happily watching the antics on the ice, the coloured lights flickering across her face.

'Look, Tash is skating with Ben,' she said, taking her drink with a nod of thanks before looking back at the rink. Following her gaze, he saw his friend was indeed entertaining Tash with some flash moves of his own. Lola's sister seemed to enjoy the attention, smiling at him surging forward, trying to outpace him as they skated around.

'I believe he would be a much better companion for

her,' he said without thinking. Lola's head snapped around, and she stared at him for a moment.

'I believe, in this instance, you are right. But she won't listen to anyone.'

'So that's genetic, huh?' he joked with a chuckle. She nudged him with her shoulder, but didn't deny it. They watched for a while, taking great entertainment from Roger's disco moves on the ice while they finished their drinks.

'Ready to go again?' Luka asked, hoping that she would. He enjoyed gazing into her eyes as he guided her around far too much.

She blew out a long breath and stood up. 'Sure, why not? Tash says it will help my skiing.'

A laugh rumbled through him as he took her hand and led her back on to the rink. 'That remains to be seen.'

Chapter Thirteen

Lola was more confused than ever. As he patiently guided her around the rink, here was good cop Luka again. Being kind and considerate and funny and all the things she liked in a man. She couldn't deny that she could fall a little in love with this side of him. His blue eyes held her attention as they skated around, making her the promise that he wouldn't let her fall, and she trusted them completely.

She couldn't help but admire his skill on the ice. Even going backwards, it was easy to see he was full of confidence and she could feel the envious glances from the surrounding women. When he suddenly let go of one hand and swooped back until he was alongside her and facing forward, she squealed in fright. But he just placed an arm around her waist and led forward with his free hand, and it amazed her to find she could do it. She was actually skating, albeit with support.

When he finally drew her to a halt next to the exit, with a question on his face, she was disappointed but laughed and said, 'yes, I think you're right. I should quit while I'm ahead.' As they made their way off of the ice, she realised he still had hold of her hand and it felt bizarrely natural. They sat and changed back into their shoes, and when they stood, he said, 'So I'll see you in the morning for your lesson. We can see if the skating helped?'

'Actually, we have a staff meeting first thing. Didn't you get the email?' She couldn't be sure, but she thought she saw a flicker of disappointment flash across his face before being replaced by his usual scowl.

'What for?' he asked grumpily. 'Don't we have enough to do without these silly get-togethers?'

And there's the bad cop, she thought with a sigh. 'There's just going to be a few changes to the schedule. There'll be coffee and croissants,' she told him in her best impression of Jolly Roger. Unimpressed, he just looked at her, his eyes filled now with disdain, and she cast her eyes back to the rink. 'Anyway,' she said quickly, 'I'm going to wait for Tash. I'll see you in the office hall tomorrow at eight.'

She turned and walked away, not able to bear the sudden contrast in his personality any longer. It was far too confusing; she never knew where she stood with the guy and it was driving her insane.

She waved at Tash the next time she and Ben came sailing past and her sister nodded in acknowledgement, reaching out a hand to pull him off the rink. They were still laughing as they got to where Lola was waiting and she watched with interest as they said their goodbyes. She could see the lovesick look in his eyes, and she wondered if her sister had any idea.

As they walked home, arm in arm, Lola mulled over how to approach the subject. Her sister got tetchy when she tried to point out what was good for her.

'Ben seems like a nice guy,' she said lightly, as they walked through the square, adding to the snowy footprints on the cobbles.

'Yeah, he's fun,' her sister replied casually. 'You seemed to be getting on OK with Luka,' she added more pointedly.

'He was very helpful,' she said primly. 'But utterly infuriating. One minute he's pleasant and the next he's snarling at me.'

Tash laughed. 'Well, you're obviously higher up in his opinion than anyone else here. We only get the snarly version. Although Ben seems to get on OK with him.'

'That's because Ben is nice. Have you two ever…'

'Don't be silly. He's a mate, that's all, and he's really not my type.'

Of course not, he's a nice guy, Lola thought, but held her counsel. When they had made it back to the cabin and were getting ready for bed, her sister asked, 'what's this meeting for in the morning?'

'Oh, just some schedule changes,' Lola replied hurriedly. 'Night, Sis.' She closed her bedroom door before she could ask anything else and dived into bed, pulling the duvet tightly around her to get warm. She knew tomorrow's news was going to be unpopular, but she was determined to shake things up and that meant keeping the kids happy. If they were happy, the parents would be, and that would all count towards her letter of recommendation at the end of the season.

She arrived early to the offices the next day to set up the coffee and croissants as promised, hoping that would go some way towards improving everyone's mood. The team shuffled in, bleary-eyed and with muttered greetings. Most of them went straight for the coffee before taking their seats. She spotted Luka at the back of the room, leaning against the wall. She smiled at him, but he just nodded curtly before looking away.

'Right, everyone,' beamed Roger, standing at the front making eye contact with them all in turn. 'We have come up with some wonderful ideas to make things even more fun for our young charges.'

They all gazed warily at him as he prattled on about the fun events that Lola had set up for the next few weeks. 'So, the bottom line is the kids' team is going to need a little help. We're going to schedule in some extra hours for you, late afternoon, to assist them. I'm sure you'll all pull together as a team to make the most of this.'

A collective groan went up from the crowd and they peppered him with questions. Lola stepped up beside him. 'Now, now. One at a time,' she called to quell the babble of voices. Steve stood up from his seat at the back. 'Yes, Steve?' she called out.

'Nothing,' he said with a shrug. 'My shop is open until 6pm, this doesn't affect me.' And he slouched out of the room. Pushing aside her dislike of the man, she gave her attention to the rest of the team, answering their questions and handing out the new rota with the extra shifts on, dreading reaching the back of the hall.

Chapter Fourteen

Luka had watched the meeting with mild amusement. He'd figured out what was coming in advance and was rewarded when the room predictably groaned in dismay, watching Lola as she deftly dealt with their queries and jollied the team along with promises of extra time off and the satisfaction of smiling little faces. He had to hand it to her. She had a way with people; he thought as she started to hand out the schedule. When she reached the back of the room, she hesitated before handing the paper to him. He scanned it quickly.

'You are joking, no?' he asked in disbelief when he saw his name highlighted against this afternoon's activity.

'I thought you'd find it preferable to the cookie decorating tomorrow,' she said with a giggle, looking at him with her sweetest face.

He sighed as he looked down at her before glancing back at the sheet. A snowman building competition, of all things. He hadn't built one since he was a child and now he had to help some annoying little brat make one. As if he didn't spend enough time with them during their lessons. Then he noticed that her name also appeared on the list for this afternoon. Maybe it wouldn't be so bad after all. He shook his head, trying to clear it of this soppy thinking, and just gave her another nod and left.

When he returned to the meeting hall that afternoon after work, Lola was there with the kids' entertainment staff and two of the lift crew who were also roped in for today.

'OK, everyone,' she called to get their attention. 'We need to get these boxes of supplies down to the square. I've raided lost and found and the kitchen for suitable things for enhancing your snowmen and I have paired you all up with a child. Please check the list before we go down so you know who you're helping.'

Luka grabbed a box and checked out the list on the board. His heart sank when he saw he had been paired up with Betty.

'Everything alright?' Lola asked, coming up and seeing his expression.

'Can I swap my child?' he asked hopefully.

'Why? What's wrong with Betty?'

'Nothing. It's her mother, she makes me... Erm, nervous.'

Lola laughed out loud. She'd seen the way the woman had been looking at him. 'I'm sure a big, strong man like you can cope with a little attention. Come on,' she called to the room at large. 'Let's get this snowball rolling!'

The team greeted this with a mix of groans and giggles, but they all took a box and trooped out and down to the square where a group of children were excitedly waiting. It was chaos for the first few minutes, but Lola soon got them organised, and when they were paired up, she stood on the podium and called out the rules.

'Right, everyone. You have half an hour to make your snowman, or woman, or even a creature if you fancy, and there will be prizes for the winners. Roger, the resort manager, will be the judge, so you need to dress your creation to impress him.'

Roger took over as Lola took her place, ready to join the activity. 'Happy building,' he called, 'On your marks. Get set, snow!'

He held up an air horn, and its blaring sound rang out. Squeals of excitement followed by a flurry of activity filled the square as the kids raced to the boxes to claim the best stuff for decorating their snowmen.

'Mr Bouchard, Mr Bouchard,' called Betty, tugging at his sleeve. 'Come on, I need you to help roll a snowball.' He didn't want to let her down, so got to action and started rolling the base. The air was filled with laughter and giggles as they all tried to keep their snowballs in one piece. Betty's face was flushed with excitement as they worked together to build up the snowman, and Luka found he was actually enjoying himself. Lola was working next to them with a small boy he didn't recognise, and he glanced over to see how they were doing.

'Call that a snowman?' she taunted, grinning at him as she worked feverishly.

'Apparently we're building a snow mummy,' he said unenthusiastically, having lost that particular argument with the young girl, and watched as Betty tried unsuccessfully to stick a pair of dangly earrings on the side of the head.

'Five minutes to go, just five minutes,' Roger called out, initiating another flurry of frantic activity. When the air horn sounded to announce the end of the competition, they all stood back, slightly breathless. Roger walked around slowly, assessing each one with a self-important air, making notes on his clipboard. With a serious face, he stood back up on the podium and grandly announced the winners.

When the snow mummy got second place, Betty screamed with joy and hugged Luka's legs ecstatically, and he gave Lola a triumphant smile. She was bent down, consoling her partner, and scowled at him over his shoulder. Betty ran over to where the parents were to find her mum, who gave Luka a flirtatious wave and a wink. He turned away and was jolted as a snowball hit him squarely in the chest. He looked down at it in surprise, wiping it away, and looked up to see Lola smirking devilishly at him.

He cocked his head to one side, a slow grin appearing as he bent down to scoop up some snow. He strolled towards her, compacting it between his hands. 'So that's how you want to play it?' he asked as she backed away from him. She shrieked and tried to duck away as he launched it at her, catching her on the shoulder. Bedlam broke out as the kids joined in, letting out whoops of joy, snowballs flying through the air as they all raced around, trying to avoid them.

'Come on, kids, let's get him!' Lola cried and they stampeded Luka. Laughing, he turned to run, but he slipped, falling to the ground. The kids piled on top of him, smushing snowballs into his face until he could barely see. Claustrophobia gripped him, the memory of being covered in snow and unable to move catching him off guard, and he rose with an angry roar.

'Enough!' he screamed. A silence fell around the square, the shocked faces of the children and accusatory looks of the adults bringing him to his senses. 'Enough,' he repeated quietly, and turned and walked away.

Chapter Fifteen

Bewildered, Lola watched Luka's retreating back. His shoulders slumped dejectedly, and he looked incredibly sad. *What the hell was that about?* She had been sure he was having a good time and couldn't understand what caused him to flip out. Noticing the muted conversations around her, she focused on some damage limitation.

'Ok, let's all go to the cafe. Free hot chocolate and cake for everyone!'

Roger came over to stand next to her as the crowd dispersed towards the cafe. 'Well done,' he said with a tight smile. 'I'm afraid I'm going to have to have a word with our resident ski instructor. Being surly is one thing, but we can't have this. Can't have this at all.'

'Roger, do me a favour and let me talk to him, please?'

He considered her for a moment. 'OK, but make it clear to him that if he behaves like this again in front of the guests, I'll have to let him go.'

Alarm ran through her at the thought of Luka leaving, followed very closely by the realisation she would miss him if he left. She checked that all the guests had gotten their orders at the cafe and were happy before thoughtfully making her way to Luka's cabin to find him. She had no idea what she was going to say, but wanted to find out what was going on with him. There must be a reason for this erratic behaviour, and she was determined to get to the bottom of it.

When he answered the door, he looked wary. His face was pinched and pale. He'd obviously just got out of the shower. His hair was still damp, sticking up in crazy directions, and she tried not to notice the fact that he only had on his jeans and his broad chest had a smattering of hair.

'Are you ok?' she asked and his face relaxed a little as he lent against the doorframe.

'I thought you were going to be angry with me.'

'I'm not thrilled,' she snorted, pushing past him into the room. He closed the door and looked at her as she stood in the middle of the room, unflinchingly staring back at him with a question in her eyes. She was mad that her special activity had been spoiled, but was more intrigued to find out what was going on with this man who baffled her so completely on a daily basis.

'You scared the life outta those poor kids,' she told him. 'The plan was to make them happy, not put the fear of God into them.' She gave him a brief smile. 'Aren't you cold?' she asked. His being half naked was very distracting, and she was struggling to concentrate. He glanced down and shrugged.

'Does it bother you?' There was a combative gleam in his eyes that made her blood start to fizz, and she looked away quickly.

'It doesn't bother me,' she said swiftly, pulling off her coat and folding it over one arm as she went to sit on the couch. 'Do you want to tell me what happened back there?'

'Would you like a glass of wine?' he asked, turning away and pulling a t-shirt off a chair and slipping it over his head.

'Sure, I'd also like you to answer the question. Roger's on the warpath.'

'I'll apologise to him in the morning,' he said gruffly, pulling the cork out of a bottle on the side and stretching up to get some glasses. His t-shirt rode up, affording her another glimpse of smooth skin, and she could feel heat rising to her face as she imagined running her hands down the dip to his waist. He poured out the wine and brought a glass over to her.

'You, I will apologise to now,' he said sincerely, handing it to her. She put her coat down beside her and took the proffered glass, taking a grateful sip. *Get a grip, Lola,* she chided herself, forcing herself to keep eye contact. 'It's my leg,' he told her, returning to the counter to collect his wine. 'I still suffer with pain from time to time and, unfortunately, today, it overpowered me. I'm sorry.'

He looked so contrite and lost, her heart went out to him. 'What on earth happened in the accident?'

Luka blinked rapidly, taking a slow sip before answering. He sat down next to her and said with a shrug, 'it was just an accident. But the x-rays of my leg looked a bit like a jigsaw puzzle. Frankly, I'm amazed they could screw any of it back together.'

'You should have told me. I mean, all of the team, not just me of course,' she stumbled on quickly. He was sitting so close she thought she could feel the heat emanating from him. The air seemed to buzz between them, and when he smiled at her, she lost her train of thought. She knew she should move away from him, away from temptation, but she was helpless against this attraction.

'As I told you before, I don't like to talk about it. I don't want people to think less of me because I have this weak point.'

'That's such a guy thing to say! It's not Achilles' heel, Luka. Nobody would think less of you because you have been through whatever it was that left your leg in a bad way.'

'You'd be surprised,' he said sharply, his face darkening with pain for a second. Impulsively, she laid her hand on his thigh.

'Nobody here would think like that.'

The air thickened around them, and they stared at each other. Lola could hear the blood pounding in her ears as bolts of electricity ran up her arm from the contact. He was impossibly close, she could just lean in and kiss him. It would take a fraction of movement to reach those lips.

Slowly, she removed her hand and leaned back, taking another gulp of wine as she pulled herself together. Lola stood and placed the glass on the coffee table, needing to put some distance between them.

'Anyway, I should go. Just make sure you see Roger tomorrow. I'll explain to him about your leg. We don't have to tell anyone else if you don't want to.'

He rose and handed her coat to her. 'Thank you, Lola. I appreciate that.'

She gave another swift smile at him and practically ran out of the door. *What the hell is wrong with me?* She thought as she scurried back down the path to the village. *I can't be attracted to Luka… can I?*

Chapter Sixteen

Luka was feeling quite rested and in much better spirits the next morning, despite yesterday's events. He had gotten a good night's sleep for once, undisturbed by the usual horrific dreams, and had woken up refreshed. The fact that meeting Lola was the first thing on his agenda added an extra spring to his step as he left his cabin.

'Good morning, Lola,' he called out when she was within earshot. She raised a limp hand in greeting but didn't respond. As he got closer, he could see she had been crying. Her eyes were red and puffy against the pale pallor of her face.

'Hey, what's up?' he asked, reaching out to touch her shoulder.

Lola sniffed and gave him a watery smile. 'It's nothing. Come on, let's get this torture started,' she joked weakly.

'Not until you tell me what's wrong,' he insisted, fighting the urge to pull her into his arms. She took a deep, shuddery breath.

'It's just... I just found out that my *abuelo*, my grandfather, he's not well. We called them this morning and my grandmother finally admitted that he has been having problems remembering things. Getting confused, you know? Apparently, the other morning he went out and got completely lost. Lost in the village he grew up in. Can you imagine? She didn't tell us before because she didn't want to worry us.'

Finally, giving in to his urge, he pulled her in and gave her a big squeeze before grasping her shoulders to hold her back slightly as he looked down at her.

'All the more reason for you to get the hang of this skiing thing, huh?'

She smiled at him gratefully. 'Yes, you're right. Let's do this!'

An hour later, Luka was happy to see Lola finally make it all the way to the base of the slope without incident. She had absolutely no grace or style, but she made it, and the smile of achievement on her face was worth every minute of the lesson.

'See, you are getting there,' he called as he walked over to join her. She grinned at him as she unclipped her skis.

'It's amazing what some extra incentive and a very patient instructor can do.'

He shook his head. 'It's all down to you, Lola, I can only point the way.'

'We both know that's not true, but thank you. Do you think I can go up to the next level tomorrow?' she asked, pointing up at the ski lifts.

A flash of a falling sensation, tortured metal squealing and screams seared through his brain, and Luka's insides twisted with fear.

'Don't be ridiculous. You barely made it down here,' he snapped at her.

Ignoring the hurt look on her face, he carried on. 'Anyway, I have to go. I will see you *here* again tomorrow morning.' And he walked away, feeling miserable and angry. None of his problems were Lola's fault, and he knew he should have been kinder to her.

Extremely thankful it was his day off, he headed back to his cabin. Yet despite his plans for a relaxing day, he could not settle. He tried to watch TV, but couldn't focus and ended up pacing the room, a jumble of thoughts and images crashing through his brain. Finally, he snatched up his phone, speed dialling the only person he could talk to when he felt like this.

'Hank, it's me,' he said when it was answered. A gruff chuckle came down the line.

'I know that. These newfangled devices have a habit of displaying your name when you call.'

Luka sank onto the couch, the sound of his old trainer's voice immediately releasing some of the pressure that had been building up inside him all morning.

'What's up, buddy? You having a tough time?'

'Something like that,' Luka replied tersely, not able to expand on the feelings that plagued him.

'Luka, I know we have talked about this before, but I'm going to ask again. Have you been to see anyone about this? To talk to someone about the problems you've had since the accident?'

'Non,' he muttered, gazing into space, absently rubbing his scar as he tried to eliminate the images that haunted him.

'Listen, I know you wear this pain like some kind of hair shirt because you feel guilty about what happened. But it was not your fault, Luka. Nobody could have predicted what happened that day. Not you, not me, not even the weathermen knew freak winds would hit the slopes like that.'

'But I made him go up. He didn't want to, and I made him. If it wasn't for me, he'd still be alive.'

'Marcel was a grown-assed man. He made his own choices.'

A silence fell between them for a moment before Hank carried on. 'It's been eight years now, son, it's time to get some help and stop torturing yourself. You're stuck in some kinda groundhog day, not allowing yourself to move forward and find happiness, maybe even love, again.'

Luka let out a bitter laugh. 'After how that woman treated me? She dropped me like a hot stone, Hank. When I was no longer the famous ski jumper, no longer the perfect arm candy to further her career.'

'Exactly. Wasn't it better to find out what she was like before you got married?'

'Hmph,' Luka conceded, slumping back against the cushions, gazing at the blank TV screen.

'I took the liberty of checking out some therapists for you. There's a really great guy based in Denver, so not too far from you. I had a chat with him about you. I'll send you his details.'

'I'm not sure there's any point, Hank.'

'Of course there is! Stop acting like a sulky teenager and grow up. The only person who can help you is yourself, so move your butt and make a phone call. What harm can it do?'

'I'll think about it.'

'Make sure you do. After all, I'm not always gonna be around to talk you off the ledge, boy. Think about that while you are at it.'

They said their goodbyes, and Luka threw his phone

onto the couch next to him. A minute later it beeped to let him know Hank had sent the details as promised. The hurt expression on Lola's face flashed before him again and he grabbed his phone and dialled the number before he could change his mind.

Chapter Seventeen

Lola was fuming. Luka's scorn had swept away the incredible high that had rushed through her body after making it down that slope in one piece in an instant. How dare he! Just when she thought she was getting the hang of it, and just when she thought she was getting to know him a little. Maybe even getting a little bit closer to him.

Stomping through the village on her way to work, grumbling to herself, she pulled up short when she spotted Steve. He was outside the hire shop with someone who was definitely not Tash, his hand rested casually on the wall as he leant into her space familiarly. The girl giggled at something he said and twirled a strand of hair as she gazed adoringly up at him. *Yup, definitely a flirting situation going on there*, she thought angrily.

'Steve,' she barked, causing him to jump back. But as he spun around, he greeted her with a smile. There was no sign of guilt on his rugged face. 'Hold on a moment, Lola,' he said and turned back and whispered something to the girl, who giggled once more and trotted off with a casual, 'see you later.'

'Now, Lola. What can I do for you?' he asked with a leery grin that made her fingers itch to slap him. Trying to control her emotions, Lola took a sharp breath through her nose before responding.

'Well, for a start. You can stop flirting with the guests, you know that's not allowed. And then you can tell my sister the truth - that you're not serious about her.'

'Oh, Tash knows we're just a casual thing,' he said glibly, seemingly unperturbed by the fierce look on her face and the anger emanating from her.

'Well, I think you had better reiterate that fact!'

He looked momentarily flummoxed. If she wasn't so mad, she would have laughed at him. 'I mean, tell her again that "you're just a casual thing." Because if you don't, I will!'

His smile faltered for a moment before he mumbled, 'whatever.' With a dismissive wave of his hand, he turned to go back into the store, making Lola's blood boil over.

'That reminds me,' she called out, matching his sly grin with one of her own as he looked back at her. 'One of the kids' entertainers is sick. I need you to help cover the disco tonight. You know, show them all the dance moves?'

Outraged, he blurted, 'but I have plans for tonight.' His tell-tale glance in the direction that the girl had just gone gave away exactly what those plans were.

'That can't be helped. And maybe it will remind you how miserable I can make your time here if you don't treat my sister right.'

He went to say something else, but thought better of it and just nodded instead and walked back into the store dejectedly.

By the time Lola got to her office, her anger had dissipated a little, and she was feeling guilty. Guilty that she had behaved unprofessionally and guilty that she had interfered in her sister's love life. Tash was going to be super mad if she found out what she had said to that insufferable man.

The morning's events left her out of sorts all day. She even snapped at Jolly Roger when he came to inquire how plans for the Lighting up Loveland ceremony were going, which made her feel worse. This is all Luka's fault, she thought, angrily slamming her laptop shut.

As if he had heard her, a text message popped up from him. She read it in disbelief. He was cancelling their lesson tomorrow morning. Not stopping to think what she was doing; she pulled her coat on and walked rapidly back through the village towards the cabins where the staff lived. The fact that it had started to snow again did nothing to alleviate her mood as she stormed up his steps and banged repeatedly on his door.

He looked sleepy and rumpled when he answered. 'Lola,' he said in surprise. 'I just sent you a message.'

'I know!' she said angrily, waving her phone at him. 'Why are you cancelling? You said you would help me. Am I that bad you think there is no hope, or are you just oblivious to how important this is to me?'

'I have to go somewhere, I have an appointment.'

'Of course you do. A magical appointment that has suddenly sprung up between this morning and now.'

'I...'

'If you don't want to help me anymore, just tell me,' she steamrollered over him. 'I'm sure I can figure out a way to do this with or without your help.'

'But, I do...'

'I thought we were friends enough by now that you could be honest and tell me the truth,' she ranted at him.

'Lola!' he shouted, finally stopping her tirade, and before she could respond, he pulled her into his arms and kissed her. There was only a second's hesitation before she returned his embrace, leaning in and deepening the kiss. The roughness of his stubble sent a delightful frisson of tingles across her skin. His scent and warmth and the feel of his lips wrapping her in a cloak of wonderful, unexpected pleasure. The unique silence caused by the blanket of snow around them made it feel like a moment trapped in time, and nothing else in the world was happening right now apart from this incredible kiss.

'What… what was that for?' she asked breathlessly when they finally pulled apart. His face creased into a grin and his blue eyes danced with amusement.

'It was the only way I could shut you up.'

'Oh,' Lola managed, her mind still befuddled and her traitorous body still fizzing with excitement.

'I really do have an appointment tomorrow morning. It's in Denver, so I have to head out early. It is in no way a reflection on my desire to help you, or my opinion on the chances of you learning to ski properly, OK?'

'OK,' she said quietly, still unable to take in the fact that she had just been thoroughly kissed.

'How about I take you to dinner tomorrow night to make up for it?' he asked, looking uncertain as he waited for her response.

'Sure,' she said, rallying a smile. 'I'd like that.'

Still in a daze, she turned and walked down the steps and towards her own cabin. She looked back. He was still there staring after her, and gave her a quick wave before going inside. A large smile appeared on her face as she looked around in amazement. How had she never noticed before how beautiful the snow made everything look?

Chapter Eighteen

The nagging tone of his alarm dragged Luka from a deep slumber the next morning. He stretched luxuriously, then remembered his appointment. Fear darted through him, bringing him upright with a start. Immediately, he decided to cancel. After all, he didn't think this doctor would be any help and there was nothing to be gained from driving the hour it took to get to Denver just to confirm that.

He swung his legs over the edge of the bed and tested his weight on his bad leg before standing and shuffling over to the kitchenette to put on some coffee. It was still early, so he could call the doctor's office and leave a message to let him know he wouldn't be coming today.

When the call was answered on the second ring, he was startled by a voice that said, 'I'm guessing this is Luka, and I'm also guessing you are ringing to cancel?'

'Dr Phillips? I didn't think anyone would be there at this hour.'

The doctor chuckled. 'Oh, the early bird catches the

worm. Or in this case, catches the patient who is too afraid to confront what he needs to.'

'I am not afraid! I just don't believe talking to you will help.'

'Well, if that's the case, there's no harm in us having a chat, is there? And at least it will get Hank off your back.'

'You have a point,' Luka conceded.

'Excellent, I'll see you at nine,' the doctor replied smartly and ended the call before he could object.

Glad to see the snow ploughs had been out after last night's heavy fall, Luka still took his time as he drove, knowing that black ice could lurk at any point to catch him out. His truck's Sat Nav guided him effortlessly to the parking lot next to the doctor's office, but he sat there for a while gazing out at nothing, trying to find the strength to go in. A momentary flash of Lola's lips on his galvanised him into action, so he locked up and made his way into the building.

As he walked through the glass doors of the two-storey office block, a man strode towards him. He was dressed in dark jeans and a t-shirt, declaring his love for AC/DC, with his blonde hair pulled back into a ponytail. He smiled warmly and stuck out his hand as he approached.

'Luka? I'm Doctor Phillips, but please call me Michael.'

Luka shook his proffered hand, gaping at him wordlessly. The doctor laughed, gesturing for him to follow. 'Not what you were expecting, huh?'

'Not really,' Luka confessed as he trailed after him through to his office. The office, like the man himself, was also not what he had been expecting. The brightly painted walls were crammed with music memorabilia, framed albums, concert posters, an electric guitar, and even a beautiful old wurlitzer jukebox, taking pride of place in one corner.

'Take a seat,' Michael said, indicating the large leather sofa, before walking over to his desk where a packet was waiting. 'Please, bear with me,' he said with a boyish gleam in his eyes. 'I just took delivery of this!' He ripped open the parcel and the plastic wrapping that held its contents. He shook out what was inside and admired it. 'Just perfect,' he said, grinning at Luka.

Slightly bemused, Luka nodded at him, unsure why a sleeping bag could cause such joy. The doctor turned and opened the built-in cupboard on the far wall, revealing a mountain of what looked like camping equipment. 'This is the Snowy Owl,' he said reverently over his shoulder. 'They use it on Polar Expeditions.' He placed it on top of a pile of boxes with Food Kits stamped on the side and closed the door. Seeing Luka's bemused expression, he chuckled.

'Don't mind me, I just like to be prepared.'

'What for?' Luka asked, thinking that this doctor that Hank had recommended to him might be just a little unhinged.

'I am a great believer in being prepared for anything life might throw at you, Luka. And this little stash, along with my music collection, will keep me going should the unthinkable happen. Would you like some coffee?'

Luka nodded as he sat, still nonplussed by the whole setup and the oddity of the man in front of him, and wondered yet again why he was wasting his time here. Once the coffee was poured, the doctor placed the mugs and a jug of creamer on the table and plonked himself happily in the big armchair that faced Luka.

'So, Luka. Tell me why you don't think you need my help,' he asked without preamble.

'No disrespect to you, doctor, I mean, Michael. But therapy is for people who are...'

'Crazy?' laughed the doctor, taking a sip of his coffee.

Ducking his head and flushing, Luka struggled for a better way of putting it. 'I mean, people who have bigger issues than me.'

'Bigger issues than, let me guess, nightmares that keep you awake for nights on end? Outbursts of anger for no reason at all, flashbacks to what happened that day, feeling sick, sweating randomly, and in pain?'

Luka glanced up at him, his mind racing. 'I guess you had a long conversation with Hank,' he said sourly.

'Not really, no,' Michael shrugged, placing his mug on the table and leaning forward earnestly, resting his elbows on his knees and clasping his hands together.

'He just told me about the accident and said you needed some help. It's not an enormous leap for me to work out the rest. I looked it up online. It was an uncommonly horrific event, Luka. There is no way *anyone* can go through something like that and not be affected in some way.'

Luka sat back, his face drawn, and blew a long breath out, trying to contain the turmoil inside him that was bubbling like a volcano about to blow.

'I'm still alive,' he spat finally. 'I have no reason to feel like this!'

'And there's the other one. Guilt.' Michael stated calmly with a nod, as if he was pleased with himself. 'And that is where I think we should start.'

The drive back to Loveland passed in a blur, Luka's thoughts replaying the conversation he'd had with Michael over and over, his emotions on a rollercoaster. He hadn't planned to get into it with the doctor, but somehow Michael had drawn him out. Snippets of thoughts and feelings that Luka had never admitted out loud in the last eight years were gently coaxed out of him. It had left him completely drained and incapable of dealing with anything else today.

But he knew he couldn't let the kids down, and his brain could probably do with the distraction. Back in his cabin, he changed into his snow gear and made his way to the meeting point, still processing the conversation from this morning. But his young charges' demands for attention soon had him focused on the job at hand, and he pushed everything else to the back of his mind for now.

When 3pm rolled around, he was happier than usual to get back home, strip off and stand under the hot jets of the shower until the water ran cold. He dried off and pulled on his comfy robe, with nothing more on his mind than stretching out on the couch to rest. He closed his eyes briefly, then sat bolt upright. Lola! He'd promised to take her for dinner. Dismissing the immediate urge to cancel - she'd be understandably mad if he did that - he forced himself to get up and dressed, because despite being as mentally and physically exhausted as he felt, he realised he really wanted to see her.

Chapter Nineteen

Lola stared at her reflection in the mirror, turning this way, then that, frowning. With a harrumph of displeasure, she ran back into her bedroom to change. Tash, who was sitting on the sofa, watching the entire process with amusement, called out, 'so this is just a casual dinner, huh?'

Sticking her head back out the door, Lola looked at her with a scowl and said firmly, 'yes! For the tenth time, yes. He just wants to apologise for letting me down this morning.' Her head disappeared again, and Tash giggled to herself, and when her sister reappeared pulling on the fourth jumper choice of the evening, she carried on teasing her.

'So why is it I haven't seen you this excited or nervous since your *quinceañera*?'

'I am not excited,' she claimed, grabbing her brush and yanking it through her long hair several times before twisting it up in a loose bun. 'I may be a little nervous. Unlike you, I don't hang out with strange men that often!'

Ignoring the insult, Tash tipped her head to one side. 'You never have really had a proper relationship, have you?

Unless there's someone you haven't told me about, of course.'

'There's been… well, stuff, you know. But no, I haven't really met anyone I have gotten close to. I guess I just haven't met the right person.'

'I'm not sure you would let him in if you did.'

Twirling around to look at her sister, Lola demanded, 'what's that supposed to mean?'

'Don't get all defensive. I just sometimes think that throwing yourself into your career, this master plan of looking after our grandparents and your constant interference in my life, is a way of avoiding getting close to anyone else.' Tash smiled to show she meant well, and Lola took a moment to consider her words.

There had been men that had wanted to take their relationship further, but Tash was right. She'd always walked away at that point, using her career and her family as an excuse to move on. But she didn't want to explore what that might mean right now. That was going to take some thinking about, and she had to get ready for this… Whatever this was.

'I'm sure it will happen one day,' she said vaguely and walked back into the bathroom to touch up her make-up. It was hard to be alluring with so many layers required, even just for the short distance she had to walk to the restaurant Luka had chosen for tonight. Finally, happy with how she looked, she left her sister grinning on the sofa and made her way thoughtfully through the village.

Her stomach swirled with butterflies as she pushed open the door of the French restaurant, a wonderful waft of garlic and herbs hitting her as she entered and immediately making her salivate. The maître d' showed her to a table at the front of the glass-enclosed terrace and took her order for a glass of wine. While she waited for Luka, she sipped on her drink and gazed out at the amazing view the terrace afforded. You could see right across the valley, and with the night approaching, lights were blinking on, twinkling in the dusk. It didn't match her ideal of the sun setting on the horizon across the ocean, but she had to admit it was pretty.

She saw Luka enter the restaurant and exchange greetings with the maître d' who pointed over to where she was sitting. As he weaved his way through the tables towards her, she noticed the unevenness of his gait, the slight favouring of his right leg.

'Is your leg bothering you?' she asked with concern when he reached her. He smiled down at her, his eyes doing that crinkling thing that was so darn cute. 'Just a little, it's nothing,' he said as he took the seat opposite her.

'So...' she said, fiddling with the napkin on the table, searching for something to say. This was the first time she had seen him since that kiss and she was feeling self-conscious.

'So?' he said, head tilted to one side, amusement playing across his features.

'Erm, how was your appointment this morning? You never said what it was for?'

His face became serious for a moment, but he was saved from answering her immediately by the waiter, bringing menus and taking his drink order, the exchange taking place in rapid French. When the waiter left, Luka seemed to have rallied.

'It went well, I think. I just needed to, shall we say, talk to someone about something?'

'Talk to someone about something? Yeah, that explains everything.'

He gave a soft laugh. 'I appreciate it sounds vague... It's

not something I want to talk about right now, but it is something that I would like to share with you when I'm ready. If that's ok with you?'

He looked so earnest, and as his eyes bore into hers, Lola squirmed in her seat. This had become pretty intense suddenly. He smiled gently, as if sensing her panic.

'So why don't you tell me about these grandparents of yours?'

Grateful for the change in topic, Lola dived in and told him about her childhood. How her grandparents had given up their retirement plans to go back to Mexico in order to look after her and her sister until they left for college. The Christmases they'd spent, usually beach-based back in Cabo, and the fun they'd had. Luka told her a little of growing up in Quebec. His American father falling for his mother, both being too involved in their careers to spend time with their son, let alone Christmas day, which had always been spent with whichever nanny was there at the time. It didn't sound like much fun to her, but she listened intently as he described his teenage years until the divorce when he chose to go with his father to continue his studies in America, winning a scholarship to further his training, and his dreams to win the Olympics.

Lola relaxed into the evening as they chatted easily, forgetting that she was here with a man she barely knew and how nervous she had been earlier. Before she realised it, they were on to the desserts and ordering coffee to finish up the wonderful meal they had shared. As he chatted away to her, she took in his handsome features. He looked so different this evening, relaxed and happy. Nothing like the grump that usually stalked about the resort.

Their easy banter faded as they walked back towards the cabins. The village was quiet now, most of the guests opting for an early night so they could try to make the first tracks in the morning. A light fall of snow was dusting everything and covering their tracks behind them.

'So, this is me,' she said nervously as they arrived at her cabin, glancing at the window to see if Tash was watching.

'Indeed, it is,' he said, gazing down at her. 'I would like to kiss you now, is that ok?' he asked huskily. Lola gave a small nod, and he pulled her towards him, cupping the back of her head and looking at her for a moment before bringing his lips to hers with the gentlest of touches. Lola melted into him, responding with more urgency, wanting to explore this explosion of sensations that his lips were creating. Sparks were fizzing through her as he traced kisses along her jaw before returning to her mouth, and she moaned quietly.

An icy hand slipping under her jumper and running up her back made her flinch, but it soon took warmth from her skin and left trails of electricity up her spine. He finally pulled away, leaving her dazed and fuzzy-headed.

'What is it about you, Lola Sanchez?' he asked in wonderment, his eyes raking over her features as if looking for answers.

'Well, I'm pretty darn cute!' she quipped, trying to control her breathing and act as if she wasn't completely blown away by this man and the havoc he caused in her body.

'Ah, that must be it,' he grinned as he checked his watch. 'I better get myself to bed. I have a lesson with a very difficult student in the morning.'

She pushed him playfully. 'Hey, you.' He gave her another, far too swift kiss, and turned and walked away, leaving her imagining him in bed and the possibility of her joining him as she made her way inside.

Chapter Twenty

There was still a bounce in Luka's step as he made his way to the beginner's slope the next morning. He'd had trouble falling asleep last night, but for once it wasn't because of the awful images that haunted him. The fact that Lola seemed to like him for who he was, rather than because he was a famous ski jumper, was tantalising. Every time he thought about her, a jolt of excitement ran through him and he had trouble keeping the grin off of his face. He didn't even mind that she turned up five minutes late for their lesson.

'Good morning, Luka,' she called breezily. 'Sorry I'm late. I had to answer a couple of urgent emails.'

'I can't imagine what is so important at this time of the morning that it couldn't wait until you get to the office.'

She tapped the side of her nose and winked. 'Just finalising the plans for our secret star to turn on the lights next week.' She chucked her skis on the ground and clipped her boots in, a look of determination on her face. 'Come on then, skiing master, make me good at this sliding down a hill thing!'

He chuckled and said, 'OK, this morning we will work on your posture.'

An hour later, he was happy to see that she had taken on board some of his teaching and was looking a little less ungainly as she made her last trip down the slope.

'I think that's enough for now,' he called as he skied down to meet her. Lola was beaming from ear to ear as she shucked her skis, and ran to give him a hug.

'Thank you, Luka, I know I still have a long way to go, but I am feeling much more confident that I will actually be able to do this silly extravaganza thing.'

'You will be fine,' he said gruffly. 'Although you are lucky, it's on the blue slope, not the black!'

She laughed in agreement. 'Yup, that's more than enough for me, thank you very much.' She glanced up at him. 'How come you never go out? Everyone else here seems obsessed with getting as much time on the slopes as possible, but I don't think I've seen you go, not once.'

His face darkened, and he turned away from her, scrambling for a plausible excuse. He couldn't tell her he was terrified of ski lifts, that despite his passion and desire to hit the slopes, he couldn't face the journey up there.

'My leg,' he said eventually, patting it to emphasise his point. 'It would put too much strain on it.'

'That's a shame. It must be hard for you to be here and not be able to enjoy it.'

He shrugged. 'It is what it is,' he said stoically. 'Come on, we both have work to do.'

As he was changing back in his cabin, his phone rang. 'Good morning, Hank. To what do I owe this pleasure?' he asked as he flicked on his coffee machine, determined to have a hit of caffeine before he faced his young charges.

'I just wanted to say well done.'

'What for?'

'For going to see Dr Phillips, of course. I didn't think you'd be up to it.'

'Well, I was, and I did,' Luka replied as he poured the coffee into his mug.

'I have to say, I'm amazed. I've been banging on about this for years. What made you change your mind?'

Lola's smiling face and her oh-so-kissable lips flashed into his mind, and he grinned. 'Let's just say I found a good reason for wanting to deal with this.'

Hank was silent for a moment. 'You've met someone.' It was a statement, not a question.

'I think I have, Hank,' Luka said happily, taking a sip from his mug.

'Does she know? Does she know what happened to you?'

The smile slipped from Luka's face as quickly as it had appeared. 'No, she doesn't. That's the beauty of it. She has no idea who I am… Who I was. She likes me for me, Hank, and that's a real novelty, as you know.'

Hank sighed down the line. 'I appreciate that, son. But I'm not so sure it's healthy. If you are really set on moving forward and putting this awful thing in the past, you have to confront it at all levels and admit what happened. It's part of who you are now.'

'Did you become a doctor suddenly?' Luka asked angrily, banging his mug on the counter, coffee slopping over the sides. 'Are you now an expert on such things?'

'I am not, Luka. Don't be mad. I'm just concerned for you, that's all.'

'Well then,' Luka said, settling a little.

'Just promise me you will talk about this with Dr Phillips next time you see him.'

'Ok, Hank,' Luka sighed. His joyous mood of earlier dissipated, and a cloud hung over him as he got ready to go and teach his first class. What if this thing with Lola was just a dream? What if she didn't want to know him when she found out the thought of going on a ski lift terrified him to the point of immobilisation, leaving him drenched in cold sweat and shaking?

He tried to push these thoughts away and focus on the lessons, but they kept encroaching despite his best efforts. What if she dropped him just like his fiance had? Would she think less of him? Walk away in disgust, thinking he wasn't a real man? He couldn't imagine kind, sweet Lola being like that, but past experience had taught him you never really know people. You couldn't trust them when it came down to it.

By the time he got home, he had come around to thinking that maybe he should end things with Lola. It was the best thing to do in the long run. The only way to keep his heart safe.

Chapter Twenty-One

Having the Lighting up Loveland event all organised, Lola threw herself into planning the rest of the itinerary leading up to Christmas. Although her mind kept drifting back to Luka and his soul-searching kisses, she couldn't help but be excited by creating this program. Her best Christmas memories from childhood involved days on the beach in Mexico with the entire family, not this cold, icy wonderland.

So bringing the magic of Christmas to life for the children staying here, as well as entertainment for the adults, was stretching her imagination and providing a much-needed distraction from everything else going on in her life right now. She was checking off her list against the calendar when Roger arrived at her door, yet again.

Barely able to keep the excitement from his voice, he asked, 'so Belinda arrives in two days?'

'Yes, Roger. She is still arriving in two days. Nothing has changed.' Lola considered him for a moment. 'Would you be able to go and pick her up from the train station when she arrives? I was going to use the regular transfer service, but I'm thinking someone this important should be met by a manager? Might be a good opportunity for some shots for Instagram!'

Roger looked like he was about to faint. Beads of sweat popped up on his forehead and he staggered slightly before turning it into a nonchalant lean against the door frame.

'I, uh… I could probably fit that into my schedule. Just send me an email to remind me of the timings.'

Lola smiled, absolutely certain that the timings were seared into his brain. 'Of course, no problem.'

Grinning to herself as she made the last couple of calls of the day, she checked her diary and realised it was the drinks mixer tonight. 'God, where did that week go?' she asked the world in general as she closed her laptop and got ready to leave. She checked her phone, frowning as she saw there were no notifications. She'd felt sure Luka would have been in touch at some point today. But then again, she hadn't been in touch with him; she chided herself as she went to get changed for the evening.

'Hey Tash,' she called to her sister, who was bent over drying her hair. 'How was your day?'

'Cold and exhausting,' Tash answered, standing back up, flicking her hair behind her.

'Ooh, you look dolled up. All for the mixer, I assume?' she smirked.

'Ha, ha, very funny. No, Steve and I are going for something to eat after putting in an appearance there.'

Not wanting to say what was really on her mind and start an argument between them again, Lola changed subjects and asked, 'did you see if the sleigh rides were running when you came in? I didn't have time to check. I might go after the drinks thing.'

'Didn't see 'em, but definitely heard the jingling of bells

and some whinnying, so I guess that's a yes. But you should go check. You can test it out with that hunky ski instructor you're *just friends with*.'

Ignoring the verbal air quotes, Lola thought about it. 'That might not be a bad idea. I'm not sure if it's Luka's cup of tea, but I did want to see what it's like. I'm thinking of adding something else to the ride. Maybe a pit stop for mulled wine or hot chocolate, something like that?'

'Good idea, sis,' Tash said, spritzing herself with perfume. 'You want to walk over to the hall together?'

Lola nodded. 'Yup, give me five minutes to change and I'll be with you.'

They walked companionably through the village, pausing to admire the sixteen-foot Christmas tree that was being installed in the square to be prepared ready for the big ceremony. When the sisters arrived at the hall, the mixer was in full swing, White Christmas blaring from the speakers and guests and staff chatting animatedly. Lola looked through the crowd, disappointed not to see any sign of Luka.

'Don't worry, he'll be here,' Tash told her with a knowing smile, rubbing her shoulder affectionately.

'Natasha, my angel,' Steve declared, sweeping her sister up and kissing her thoroughly. His eyes flicked defiantly over to Lola and away again. Fuming inside, Lola strode over to the bar, determined not to let that man rile her into saying something stupid in front of Tash. As she waited for her drink, she became aware of Luka standing next to her. She felt his presence and recognised his cologne before he even uttered a word.

'Hey, Lola. How are you?'

She turned to look up at him, butterflies cavorting

through her stomach as she met his eyes. He looked serious, despite his effort to smile, subduing her initial excitement.

'I'm good, thanks. I had a productive day. You?' she queried, searching his face, wondering what had made him look so solemn. This morning he had been quite cheerful, but now there was an air of melancholy about him.

'Oh, you know. Lots of small people falling over and demanding my attention. You know how it is,' he said lightly, the smile still not reaching his eyes. 'Listen, I wanted to have a talk with you, away from this,' he said, raising his brows at the surrounding festivity.

A knot of concern formed in her stomach. She had no idea what he wanted to talk about, but her senses were flashing red alert at his tone.

'I had planned to go and check out the sleigh ride after this. I have some ideas to make it even more special, but I need to see it in action first. You can come with me to that of you like,' she rambled on. 'It might be fun, you never know…' she petered out under his gaze, watching as he considered the idea and finally nodding.

'OK, we can do that,' he announced, sounding for all the world like he'd rather poke himself in the eye than spend time with her on a romantic sleigh ride through the snow. Heart sinking, Lola took a sip of her drink as she turned to face the crowds. This was why she didn't get involved. It was too complicated, too distracting, and she needed to concentrate on furthering her career. Not worry about what was going through the minds of men she couldn't read or understand.

She sighed, watching as Tash and Steve twirled around the dance floor laughing, and she couldn't help but notice Ben on the side-lines looking dejected. Why can't I find something like that, she wondered as she watched the happy couple. Despite her poor choice in men, Tash always seemed to enjoy herself, living in the moment, not thinking about what tomorrow would bring. Lola found it impossible to be that carefree. Her responsibilities to her family weighed heavily, and she wished fervently that she could cut loose for once and just have some fun.

Chapter Twenty-Two

Going on a sleigh ride wasn't the ideal way to tell Lola that he thought they shouldn't explore their budding relationship any further, but he couldn't think of what else to suggest. Especially now, he thought, as he watched her from the corner of his eye. She was looking at the dance floor, a faint smile on her lips, eyes lit up by the flashing disco lights, and she looked too beautiful for words. He gulped back a wave of emotion with a mouthful of scotch and ordered another to bolster his resolve. The jumble of thoughts continued to cloud his brain as they stood in strained silence, watching the party evolve around them.

'Shall we go?' Lola asked suddenly, as if she couldn't bear to be here anymore.

'Of course,' he agreed, and they walked to the exit, picking up their coats and scarves from the foyer and wrapping up tight before venturing outside. The air was crisp, their breath coming out in foggy plumes as they walked down the slope to where the ponies were stabled.

'So, you have plans to improve the ride?' he asked, to

break the silence that had remained markedly between them.

'Yes. I mean, it is hugely popular from what I can see from the previous years' customer surveys, but I always like to push things one step further. Try to add a little extra, especially as we have so many repeat guests. It gives them something new to experience.'

'Change isn't always good,' he grumbled at her. 'Some people like things just the way they are.' His foot slid out from under him and he stumbled, an unmanly yelp leaving his lips. He stood for a moment, waiting for the pain to subside.

'Are you ok?' Lola asked, her face etched with concern. *I should say something*, Luka thought, his brain scrambling wildly. But before he found the words to express what was on his mind, another voice called out.

'Hey, Lola, have you come for a ride?' Chad Sharman, the manager of the stables, loped over. He was a tall, lithe man with a bushy moustache nestled above a huge grin, and he had a strong air of confidence about him. 'I was waiting to see if we get any more takers after the mixer, but you can take the last ride out if you like?' he asked cheerily.

'That's exactly why I'm here, Chad, thank you,' Lola replied. Her eyes shining with excitement as she hurried towards where the carriage was waiting, the tethered pony stomping its feet as if impatient for the off.

Luka found himself dragged along by her enthusiasm, and before he knew it, he was cosied up under a blanket in a horse-drawn carriage, rumbling across the snow at a tidy pace. The gentle tinkle of the bells on the harness matched the rhythmic stride of the horse as it trotted along the path and across into the woods. Giving in to the moment, he leaned back, letting his head rest on the seat, and looked up at the stars. Seeming to sense his relaxation, Lola snuggled into him, and his arm naturally fell over her shoulders, pulling her in closer.

'You seem a little out of sorts tonight. Is everything ok with you?' Lola asked quietly. Luka looked down at her. She was biting her lip and her face creased with worry. His gut twisted at being the cause. Hank's words came back to taunt him. Maybe he should tell her what he had been through? His mind baulked at that idea. He wasn't ready to talk about that with her. But maybe he could share something, rather than just running away?

'Lola, the thing is… '

'What, Luka, please just tell me what's wrong?'

'I like you… I like you a lot, and the thing is, the last time I liked someone, I got hurt badly.'

Lola tilted her head to one side, a small smile playing around her lips, but she asked seriously, 'do you want to tell me about it?'

'Yes… no. I don't know.' he mumbled. She reached up and kissed him gently, flooding his mind with blessed peace from its chaotic thoughts and relaxing the tension in his body.

'I think I should tell you some of it, so you can understand why I'm a little weird sometimes.'

'That would be very helpful,' she grinned at him. 'But only if you want to.'

Closing his eyes, he rested his head back against the seat. 'I was in love, engaged. We were going to get married in the New Year.'

Taking his cue, Lola snuggled back into his armpit, as if she was listening to a bedtime story. 'So what happened?'

'The accident happened.' He chuckled mirthlessly; eyes still closed.

'What happened exactly?'

'That's not relevant right now, although rather ironically, next week marks the eighth anniversary of that particular event. Anyway, I'd been in the hospital for about two weeks before she finally came in to see me. To tell me it was over, that I was no longer what she was looking for in a husband, and everything I believed we had as a couple was a complete illusion.'

Chapter Twenty-Three

Lola bolted upright in shock, anger flowing through her that someone could be so cruel, so downright selfish. To abandon him in his hour of need like that was just unthinkable to her. She had never been even close to wanting to marry anyone, but she had always assumed that when she did, it would be the real deal.

'Oh my God, how could she do that?' she demanded in horror. His head still rested on the back of the seat, but his eyes slid open, staring up at the starry sky.

'I have no idea. Believe me, I have thought it through from every possible angle, but none of the solutions present her in a good light. And that's what's so hard to accept of someone you loved, that they were so completely flawed and you didn't see it. It makes you doubt yourself. It makes you doubt, when you finally meet someone else you feel a connection with, that it could possibly be real.'

His eyes finally came to meet hers and she understood the confusion and awkwardness that she saw there. No wonder the poor guy had issues, and here she had thought that she was the one with emotional baggage. She saw his eyes look off to the side and widen in astonishment.

'Look, a shooting star.' he said in delight, raising his arm to guide her.

She followed the direction of his pointed finger and saw the tail end of its trail disappearing over the horizon, perfectly highlighted by the dark, silken sky.

'Time to make a wish, Luka,' she whispered with a smile and he grasped her face with his gloved hands and kissed her fervently. She responded in kind and was soon lost in him, wanting to kiss away his pain and erase what that woman had done to him. Her mind was still reeling at the staggering cruelty of those actions, and she felt the intrinsic need to protect him from further harm.

They were interrupted when a discreet cough alerted them to the fact that they had stopped and were back in the village; they both came up for air, looking slightly bewildered.

'Sorry to interrupt,' but I need to get this 'ol girl back into her stable and rubbed down for the night,' Chad grinned, with a glance at the pony. Sheepishly climbing down from the carriage, Lola arranged with Chad that she would come by the next day and discuss her plans for additions to what she now knew was a magical ride.

They walked back to her cabin, hand in hand, stopping at intervals to kiss again, the journey taking twice as long as it should, but neither of them caring.

'Thank you, Luka,' she said when they finally reached her door. 'Thank you for sharing that with me. I appreciate it must have been tough for you'

He shrugged off her words, kissing her deeply again. 'I will see you in the morning for your lesson, yes?'

'Sure,' she smiled up at him. 'I'm up for some more torture!'

She was grinning like the Cheshire cat as she unlocked the front door, but it faded when she realised that it was all dark inside and Tash wasn't back yet, not liking the thought that her sister was still gadding about with that man. Deciding to distract herself by making some hot chocolate, she sat at the table and opened up her laptop. A few minutes of checking her emails and scrolling through her Instagram feed failed to keep her interest, and on impulse she Googled Luka's name and typed the word accident after it.

The results came in thick and fast. She opened up the images in another tab; her face a rictus of horror at the aftermath caught on camera. There was even shaky video footage, captured with phones by onlookers, their shocked expletives crudely bleeped out.

When Tash eventually came home, she found her sister sitting at the dining table, whey-faced, eyes still wide in horror. Dropping her coat to the floor, she rushed up to her.

'Lola, what's wrong? Has something happened?' When Lola didn't respond, she shook her shoulder and asked her again. 'What is it?'

Silently she turned her laptop so Tash could see the screen and the reams of news footage. Lola clicked on another tab so her sister could read the detailed article she had found. Tash's eyes flicked through the first few lines, then she slumped down in shock on the chair next to Lola.

'Oh. My. God,' she said, still reading avidly. 'This is absolutely horrific. No wonder the guy is so grumpy and never goes skiing,' Tash stated, her eyes still scrolling down.

'It gets worse,' Lola said tightly, hands clenched into fists on the table.

Tash's head snapped round. 'Worse than your ski lift being flung off the tracks by high winds, killing your team-mate and leaving you in a thousand pieces?'

'Get to the bottom bit, about his fiancé leaving him.'

Tash read on, her eyes widening further as she reached the end. She swivelled around to face her sister and they stared mutely at each other. 'This calls for alcohol,' Tash stated, standing and striding into the kitchen to grab some wine and two glasses. She waved the bottle wildly at Lola. 'You have to warn him,' Tash said. 'You have to tell him tomorrow!'

Lola shrank into her seat, her eyes wild and scared. 'I didn't know,' she moaned. 'How was I to know?'

Splashing two healthy measures of wine out, Tash shoved a glass into her hand. 'You weren't to know Lola, but you have to tell him. You have to warn him that his evil, shallow ex-fiancé is coming to Loveland in two days' time!'

Chapter Twenty-Four

Back in his cabin, Luka poked the glowing embers that remained of the fire he had lit earlier until they sparked back into life. Tossing some kindling on top and blowing on it until he was sure it had caught; he went to the kitchen and poured a glass of red wine before settling on the sofa to enjoy the warmth and the flickering flames.

He felt lighter somehow, his mind less chaotic. Maybe there is something in this unburdening yourself theory after all, he thought, while sipping his wine. His next appointment with Dr Phillips was tomorrow afternoon, and while he wasn't necessarily looking forward to it, the looming appointment no longer terrified him. He sat there until the flames died down again, a rare sense of contentment keeping him up much later than usual.

The following morning, he bounded out of bed, humming to himself as he showered and got ready to meet Lola. This was the happiest he had felt in a long time, and the constant smile on his face was making his cheeks ache. He couldn't believe how meeting Lola had turned his mood around in such a brief space of time. It was nothing short of miraculous and he couldn't wait to see her.

He saw Lola was there already waiting for him at the top of the slope, and he jogged the last few steps to envelop her in a hug. She was rigid in his arms, and he leaned back to look at her. She looked dreadful, mauve smudges under her eyes revealing lack of sleep, and her eyes skittered around, unable to meet his.

'What's wrong, Lola? Has something happened to your grandfather?' he asked, shifting his head around in front of her to try to catch her eyes. She shook her head mutely, finally allowing their gazes to lock.

'I have to tell you something,' she whispered, her voice sounding hoarse.

Luka's stomach plummeted to his boots, a sense of impending doom washing over him.

'Ok...' he said, drawing out the small word as if it would delay what was coming.

'You know I said I had arranged for someone else to turn on the lights, you know, for the big ceremony?'

'Sure I do. It's a good idea.'

'I thought so. But you have to understand, I didn't know you see...' she pleaded. 'I picked someone because I knew Roger liked her, that's all.'

He shook his head in confusion, but an unsettling inkling was trying to get his attention at the back of his mind. 'Get to the point, Lola,' he said gravely, dropping his arms and stepping away from her.

She looked down at her boots and mumbled something unintelligible.

'For goodness' sake, speak up and spit it out!'

Head still bowed, she looked up through her lashes at

him. 'It's Belinda. It's Belinda who is coming to turn on the lights.'

He took another step back, as if he'd received a physical blow, his face contorting into an ugly grimace.

'Well, she can't,' he snapped, starting to pace. 'She can't come here. I'm not sure what I would do if I saw that woman again.'

'But it's all arranged,' Lola said, watching him stalk up and down, leaving a trail in the snow.

'So just un-arrange it. Get someone else, anybody else,' he replied, his voice getting louder and harsher with each word.

'Luka, I can't. It's too late, and besides, Roger wouldn't want anyone else.'

'You could tell him she cancelled! Make up an excuse, I don't know. You're the creative one. Come up with something.'

She stared at him, lost for words, until finally she took a deep breath and said, 'you know how important this entire season is to me. And getting Belinda to turn on the lights is a real coup.'

He stopped pacing and glared at her, unable to believe what he was hearing. 'More important than my feelings?' he asked in a low voice, trying to hold back the anger that was threatening to erupt.

'That's not what I mean,' she cried. 'It's just there is nothing I can do now.'

'You mean there is nothing you want to do. You mean that this ridiculous event is far more important than any feeling I may have on the matter? At least I know where we stand,' he said coldly and turned and walked away.

'Luka! Luka, come back,' she called, but he ignored her cries and kept going. He wanted to get as far away from her as possible. Anger coursed through him. He'd been duped yet again. Why was he attracted to women who cared more about their careers than him? He should have followed his instincts and just finished it with her while he'd had the chance, before he opened up and allowed himself to believe that they had something special. That she might actually love him for who he was. But she obviously didn't care at all. That much was clear.

He slammed the door of his cabin shut, making the windows rattle, and stood staring at the wall, unsure what to do next. He flexed his fingers. The urge to hit something was overwhelming, but he grabbed his keys instead and headed out to his truck. It was far too early to go to Denver, but he needed to get out of Loveland, away from everything that was causing him so much pain.

The heavy clouds above looked like a rolling wall of fog, and as he drove out of the village, it started to snow. The stormy sky suited his mood, and he drove on regardless of the warning signs flashing over the highway of the incoming bad weather. It reduced traffic to a crawl as he neared Denver, but he was still several hours early for his appointment when he pulled up in the parking lot. He turned off the engine and a pristine white covering soon obliterated his windscreen.

The warmth of the cabin was rapidly dissipating, the air taking on a warning chill, and he knew he would have to find somewhere else, somewhere warmer, to wait. Locking the truck, he trudged down the street feeling numb, and went into the first coffee shop he could find.

Chapter Twenty-Five

Lola didn't know how long she stood there staring in the direction that Luka had taken. She also didn't know how things could have gone so wrong so quickly, but they had. She had finally met a man she felt a genuine connection with, one that she actually wanted to move forward with, to see if this relationship could be something. But now? Now he was gone, and she had a feeling there was no coming back from this. Tears trickled from the corners of her eyes, and the cold tracks they left down her cheeks alerted her to the flurries of snow silently falling around her.

She gave herself a shake, wiped away the tears, and wrapped her scarf tighter around her neck before trudging down to the village. She walked towards the bakery, feeling the need for some hot chocolate to warm her up and soothe her heart, bumping into Steve as he bustled out, croissant in hand.

'Ah, the other beautiful Sanchez sister,' he exclaimed, holding the door open for her with a flourish.

'Why haven't you ended things with Tash?' she

demanded, her emotions getting the better of her. 'I thought I made it quite clear that I could be quite vindictive with my event scheduling if I had to.'

He took another bite of his croissant, crumbs collecting in his beard, nodding thoughtfully as he chewed. 'That you did, Lola. But the thing is, you can only do that if you are still the Events Coordinator.' He grinned his infuriating, crooked grin, the crafty gleam in his eyes riling her even further.

'What are you going on about?' she asked angrily. She really didn't need his nonsense right now. She just wanted to get her drink and go and hide in her office.

'I am going on about the fact that one of the stipulations of working here is the ability to ski,' he said triumphantly. 'And I happen to know that you are sadly lacking in that department.'

Lola hadn't thought she could feel any worse today, but her stomach dropped sickeningly and her heart rate spiked alarmingly. 'I'm not sure where you acquired that snippet of information, but you shouldn't believe everything you hear,' she said as calmly as she could.

'Are you saying your sister is a liar?' he asked, looking irritatingly pleased with himself. *Oh Tash*, she thought, *what am I going to do with you?*

'I think she was pulling your leg, Steve. And if you think that would stop me telling her what a sneaky, two-timing rat you are, then you are very much mistaken,' she replied haughtily and pushed past him into the warmth of the bakery. Her hands were shaking as she took the takeaway cup from the smiling woman that ran the place, and the first sip tasted bitter, not comforting at all.

When she finally got to her office, she abandoned the hot chocolate, shrugged off her coat and slumped into her chair. She folded her arms on the desk and lay her head there, allowing the tears to come. The stress of worrying about her grandfather and losing her job was nothing compared to the pain she felt now. The image of Luka's face lit up in wonderment at the sight of the shooting star last night came back to haunt her.

He had looked so hopeful, so happy, and she had been the reason for that. She knew that with certainty, the intensity of his kisses had made that plain. It had given her a spark of hope that despite what her sister had said about her being closed off and not letting people in, that she was capable of falling in love. But here she was, alone again, with nothing but her career and her grand plan to keep her warm. The sound of someone in the hallway made her sit up, and she roughly swiped her face with her sleeve as Roger came in, a chirpy smile on his face.

'Tomorrow is the big day!' he announced happily, unaware of her distress. 'I take it everything is going to plan?'

'Yes, Roger. Everything is going to plan,' she said tiredly. 'Belinda will arrive, turn on the lights, and kick off the festive season.'

'You don't sound very excited,' he said, squinting down at her. 'Are you alright? You look a little peaky.'

'I'm fine, Roger,' she replied, rubbing the side of her face. 'Just a bit under the weather, maybe coming down with something.'

'Well, we can't have that. Can't have that at all. Our amazing new Events Coordinator needs to be on top form. I tell you what, get yourself home, take the rest of the day off. You'll be as good as new in the morning, ready for our illustrious guest.' He beamed affably at her, bobbing his head in approval at his own suggestion.

'Thanks, Roger. I think I'll take you up on that,' she said, pushing her chair back and standing.

'Good, good. A bit of rest and relaxation is just the ticket. I'll see you tomorrow,' he trilled excitedly and walked back up the hall. When she got back to the cabin, it surprised her to find Tash was there getting changed out of her work clothes.

'What's up?' she asked. 'Do you have the day off as well?'

'They've closed the slopes. The weather's too bad,' her sister said happily, then frowned. 'What are you doing here?'

'Things didn't go well with Luka,' she said, flopping onto the couch. 'Roger thinks I'm ill and sent me home.' She gave a wan grin at Tash, who was pulling her shoes on. 'Where are you off to?'

'To hang out with Steve, but never mind that. Are you OK?'

'I really wish you wouldn't hang out with that man,' Lola said angrily, standing and yanking off her coat. 'I am pretty sure you are not the only one he's messing around with, Tash. He will only break your heart.'

Tash glared at her, then carried on getting ready to leave, pausing at the door. 'Just because your love life is up the spout doesn't mean you have to take it out on me!'

And with that, she was gone. Leaving Lola to sink back onto the couch with a heavy heart and no idea what she should do to fix this mess.

Chapter Twenty-Six

Luka was on his third cup of coffee and pretty wired when Michael dropped onto the stool next to him, startling him out of his reverie.

'Hey, Luka. What are you doing here?' he asked, waving at the server for a coffee for himself. 'Most of my clients have cancelled today. The weather is pretty intense, huh?' he asked with a glance out of the window. He wrapped his hands around the mug placed before him, warming them for a moment before taking a hearty sip, eyes still on Luka.

'I came early,' he said grimly, staring blindly at the wall behind the counter.

'That I can see. I'm just wondering why?' the doctor said cheerfully. 'I mean, I know I'm fun to be around, but people don't usually turn up...' he glanced at his watch, 'three hours early to meet me.'

'Actually, it was more like five hours early,' Luka told him with a humourless smile.

'Hmm,' Michael muttered with a thoughtful sip. 'Now, I could be wrong, and it could be my amazing personality that has brought you here, but my senses tell me you need to talk?'

'I just had to get away,' Luka replied, finally meeting the doctor's eyes.

'Fair enough. Although, in my experience, running away rarely solves anything, certainly not in the long run. But you ended up here, which is a good sign. How about we get these to go, and take a walk to my office?'

Luka nodded and stood silently while Michael organised their drinks, then followed him as he led the way out of the coffee shop and up the snow-covered street. The snow was still falling heavily and there were few people out and about. Just the odd scurrying figure passed them, head down, focused on getting home, no doubt, and out of the wind and the cold. The office felt warm as they entered, but Michael still paused and turned the thermostat up a notch before slipping off his coat.

'Can't stand the cold,' he grinned. 'Make yourself comfortable.'

Luka took his coat off and sat on the edge of the couch, looking around at the memorabilia.

'You really like music, don't you?'

'Doesn't everyone?' he asked, sitting opposite Luka on the same chair as last time. When Luka didn't respond, he leaned forward, looking straight into his eyes. 'Do you want to tell me what's going on?'

Luka stared back at him, uncertain where to start. How could he describe the betrayal he felt from a woman he had only just met? Now he came to put it into words, it didn't make any sense. Let's face it, he and Lola barely knew each other, so why he felt this much pain at her actions he didn't understand.

'Usually, it's best to start at the beginning,' Michael said gently, with his usual clairvoyance.

So Luka did. Slowly at first, hesitantly describing how Belinda had walked out on him after the accident, something he hadn't mentioned last time he was here, then speeding up as he described Lola and how she made him feel. How she had awakened something in him that he never thought he would experience again, and how being with her had given him a semblance of peace for the first time in so long, that he had allowed himself to believe it was real until this morning.

'So, you see, I can't understand why I feel so devastated. It's not like last time. I was with Belinda for years. We were going to get married, for God's sake.' Luka finally collapsed back into the couch, exhausted by all the emotions crowding his mind.

'It makes perfect sense to me,' Michael said casually, standing and collecting their now empty cups and popping them in the trash can by his desk.

'Really?' Luka asked, his voice laced with sarcasm. 'Please do tell.'

Michael sat back down, and laser-focused his stare on him. 'Luka, everything you're feeling is completely valid.'

Luka sat forward again, head tilted to one side. 'How so? You mean it is right that I feel so betrayed by Lola over this?'

'No, that's not what I meant. When all this happened, the accident, Belinda walking out on you, all that stuff. You never dealt with it. You shoved everything you were feeling deep inside and out of sight. These feelings that have emerged now are latent emotions that have been lurking away, waiting for the right catalyst to bring them to the surface.'

Luka shook his head in confusion. 'I don't understand, Michael, are they valid or not?'

'Oh, they are valid,' the doctor replied cheerily. 'You're just aiming them at the wrong person.'

Slowly leaning back, Luka took in the words, trying to make sense of them. Finally grasping at the point, he asked, 'so all this anger I feel towards Lola is actually my anger for Belinda?'

'By jove I think he's got it!' the doctor parodied shamelessly.

Wordlessly contemplating the smiling doctor, Luka's brain ran through the scene this morning and his reaction to Lola's plea's that she didn't know and couldn't change it, the anguish etched on her face. He stood abruptly.

'I have to get back.' He grabbed his coat and looked at Michael. 'I have to get back and make it right with her.'

'I totally agree,' the doctor replied, standing next to him. 'But look out there, it's a blizzard. You can't possibly go out in that.'

Pulling on his coat with a grim look of determination, Luka gave a manic grin.

'Just watch me.'

Chapter Twenty-Seven

Lola woke up with a start. She had fallen asleep on the couch and her sister was banging the kitchen cupboard doors with pointed force. She rubbed her eyes and sat up, bending her head from one side to the other in an effort to relieve the stiffness in her neck. The scanty light coming through the window indicated it was still very early and her head remained fuzzy despite the sleep.

'What's up with you?' she asked as Tash pulled out a mug and banged it on the counter. Her sister turned and glared at her.

'I hope you're happy!' she snarled, turning back to pour some coffee, slopping it onto the counter. 'Steve and I broke up.'

Lola took a minute before responding. She was delighted with this news, even in her sorry state, but her sister obviously was not, and she had to tread carefully.

'I'm sorry, Tash,' she said, standing up and dumping her blanket on the couch. 'But maybe it's for the best?'

Tash remained resolutely facing away from her, her

back stiff, anger emanating in palpable waves as she slurped on her coffee.

'Why did you have to interfere?' she demanded. 'I asked him about what you said, about him seeing other people, and that's not true. He told me he only wanted to be with me, but he has to break it off because you threatened him with all sorts of nonsense.'

'That's not what happened,' Lola said quickly, walking over to her.

'Did you, or did you not make him cover the kids' disco the other day?'

'Well, yes, but… '

'And did you or did you not tell him you would schedule him in for more activities like that if he didn't break up with me?'

'That's not exactly what happened,' Lola said, pulling her sister around to face her. 'I saw him, Tash. I saw him chatting up one of our guests.'

'Yes, he told me you got the wrong idea about that. He was just helping her with snowboard hire, doing his job, and you just assumed the worst and went mental on him.'

Lola ducked her head, trying to catch her sister's eyes as she stared over her shoulder, refusing to meet them. She could see she had been crying, and it pained her to know this was her doing, even though it was for the best in the long run.

'Please believe me when I tell you that is not how it was.'

'All I know, Lola, is that I was very happy, and now, because of you, I'm not. So forgive me if I find it hard to believe anything you say.' With that, she drained the last of her drink, dumped her mug in the puddle on the counter, and stormed out of the door.

'Well, that's just perfect,' Lola said to the empty room. 'I didn't think today could be any worse than I imagined, but here we are.'

She took a long shower, trying to wash away the awful feeling that gripped her. Everything was going wrong, and she had to get through what should have been a triumphant day by feigning enthusiasm for the lighting up ceremony. As she left the cabin, on impulse, she turned away from the route to the office block and walked around to Luka's cabin. She could see his truck wasn't there and her heart sunk further. She knocked on his door anyway, but nothing but silence answered her.

Yesterday's storm had left banks of snow piled up along the path to her office. It was still early, but she could see the ground staff were out with buckets of salt, trying to clear the way. They had their work cut out for them today. The sky was still heavy with threatening, ugly clouds, and a chilly wind whipped her hair about her face as she trudged along. When she got to the office, she hung up her coat, rubbing her hands together to try and bring the feeling back to them. Her brain was scrambling with ideas. How could she fix this mess?

She pulled her phone from her bag and dialled Luka's number, but it went straight to voicemail. She had no idea what to say, so she killed the call without leaving a message. *Where the hell was he?* She thought, terrified that he had left for good and she would never get the chance to make things right with him. Surely this couldn't be the end of it. Tears welled up again, and she swiped them away angrily. All she wanted was to feel him in her arms again and let him know what he truly meant to her.

Chapter Twenty-Eight

When Luka left Denver, he was fired up with a desperate need to get back to Loveland and back to Lola. Michael had tried to talk him out of it, but he wouldn't listen, determined to make the journey despite the terrible weather and the night approaching. The doctor had insisted on giving him some of his supplies and loaded up Luka's truck with the contents of his emergency cupboard, a self-satisfied gleam in his eyes.

When his truck ground to a halt, defeated by the towering snow drifts just a few miles down the highway, Luka gave silent thanks to the man. He sat there drumming the steering wheel with an urgent tattoo, debating his next move. He didn't have much choice, and it was driving him insane. His phone was completely dead, so all he could do was wait it out until the roadside assistance patrol came by.

He peered out of the side window, but the ongoing blizzard obliterated everything, and he didn't hold out much hope of being rescued anytime soon. Slumping back into the seat, he checked the fuel gauge. He had just under a quarter of a tank so he could leave the engine idling for a while to provide much needed warmth, but he had no idea how long it would last. He placed his hands on the wheel and rested his head there, trying to still the cacophony of thoughts swirling around his mind.

He had no one to blame for his current situation but himself. If he had confronted Belinda all those years ago, if he had listened to Hank and gone to get help after the accident, none of this would have happened. He beat his head against his hands, trying to stop the onslaught. He couldn't bear to think how Lola was feeling right now. She must hate him. His overreaction to her booking Belinda to turn on the lights was inexcusable, and he doubted she would ever forgive him.

He didn't know how long he sat there feeling sorry for himself, but a noticeable drop in temperature despite the heater running let him know that night was falling, and a glance at the gauge again told him it had dropped a few points. He shook his head, trying to clear it and focus on the issue at hand. Realistically, he could be stuck here all night as the storm showed no sign of abating, so he needed to conserve the fuel to try to eke it out as long as possible.

He twisted around and rummaged through the supplies that the doctor had hastily piled up behind his seat. Pulling out the thermos of coffee, bottles of water and some protein bars, he finally found what he was looking for: the Snowy Owl sleeping bag. Happy that it would keep him warm enough for a while, he pushed the seat back and struggled to slide his legs into it, lifting himself up to slide it up his body and zipping it up, all the while wondering at the irony of it being named after his home country's national bird. That done, he turned off the engine and settled down as best he could to wait for rescue.

The night dragged on. Luka dozed intermittently, waking with a start each time, hoping he heard sounds of rescue, but he was still alone in his snowy tomb. Fighting to keep those grim thoughts at bay, he settled back down and drifted off again. Muffled voices woke him and, opening his eyes, he could see a muted brightness through the casing of snow. Struggling into a sitting position, he called out. 'Here! I'm in here!'

There was a distant scraping sound and finally a sliver of light found its way through a hole in the snow covering his window. A face peered through. The man turned and called something to whoever was behind him and his face disappeared. It was soon replaced by a snow brush which began to clear the window. The man peered in again. 'You OK?' he shouted. Luka gave him a thumbs up and a small smile, the relief that someone had finally come to help him leaving him weak and wordless. He unzipped the sleeping bag and shuffled out of it while he waited for them to get him free.

When they finally managed to free up the door, they wrenched it open and helped him out. He was a little unsteady on his feet as he was guided to an ambulance, waiting to check the condition of people stranded. As he sat in the back, he could see through the open doors that the weather still looked ominous. The highway had been ploughed; the snow banked up on the sides in enormous piles, the grubby tracks on the road showing evidence of traffic.

'Is the road clear?' he asked the paramedic, checking his blood pressure. She glanced up with a shrug. 'For now, it is. But I'm not sure how long it will last. The storm is coming back around again.'

Chapter Twenty-Nine

Lola went down to the square to oversee the final decoration of the enormous tree taking pride of place in the centre. The ground staff crew were hustling about, trying to get everything done despite the copious amounts of snow they had to deal with. Some of the previously hung decorations and lights had fallen with the weight of the snow overnight, so they had to be rehung.

The band booked to play tonight arrived to do their soundcheck and Roger sent her a delighted message to let her know that despite the delays this morning, Belinda's train would arrive soon. As she watched her team scramble to get everything done, the icy wind whipped around them and her heart went out to them in gratitude.

Deciding that they all deserved a warming drink, she walked up the side of the square and entered the bakery. Liz was behind the counter and smiled at her request.

'Leave it with me, Lola. I'll get the girls to bring out trays as soon as it's ready.'

As she left, she saw Ben, who was heading out of the village towards the lower slopes.

'Good morning, Lola!' he called out and walked over to see her. 'How are you today? I see everything is looking good for tonight.'

She gave a noncommittal shrug and mustered a smile. 'We should be ready in time for the big ceremony. Are you off to work?'

He nodded happily. 'Yes, Tash just called. Apparently someone called in sick, so she needs me to help her man the lifts up on the black slopes.'

'How did she sound?' she asked him, wondering if her sister still hated her.

'Er, OK, I guess. Why, what's up?'

'Oh, we just had a fight, that's all. Actually, can you do me a favour and keep an eye on her today? She and Steve broke up, and she's not in the best place right now.'

Ben couldn't contain the delighted grin that sprung to his face at this news. 'Oh dear. What a shame,' he said unconvincingly. 'Don't worry, I'll look after her.'

He hurried off with new vigour in his pace and Lola hoped her sister had the sense to see what was right beneath her nose. Back in the square, she called the crew in for a break, and as they gathered around her, the girls from the bakery arrived bearing trays of steaming hot chocolate. When the break was over, they all got back to work and Lola helped add the last decorations to the tree.

Standing back to watch as they carefully manoeuvred the star into place at the very top, she felt a thrill of satisfaction shoot through her. Despite the drama of everything going on in her life, the square looked exquisite, the perfect picture of Christmas.

Calling out her thanks to the teams as they collected up

the ladders and debris from the decorating, she made her way back to the office. She took out her phone and dialled Luka's number again, unsurprised that it still went straight to voicemail.

'Luka, it's me. Where are you? Look, I know you're mad, but please let me know that you're OK?' her voice cracked, and she took a sharp breath to steady it. 'If you don't want to talk, just send a message - anything to stop me from worrying about you.'

Sitting behind her desk, she opened her laptop, hoping to distract herself with work, but her thoughts kept wandering off, worrying about Luka. When her phone chimed an incoming message, she lept on it, almost knocking it to the floor in her haste. But it was from Roger, announcing he had safely delivered their star to her cabin and he was coming to the office to talk to her about something. Lola frowned at the tone of his message. She'd thought he would be full of excitement, but he sounded anything but.

He arrived a short while later, a serious expression on his usually genial face. 'Can I have a word, Lola?' he asked and walked up to his office, leaving her to follow, perplexed, in his wake. He sat behind his desk and gestured for her to take a seat.

'I'll get straight to the point, Lola,' he said, looking flustered and staring at her with a peculiar expression. 'It has been brought to my attention that despite your wonderful abilities as Event Coordinator - which really are top-notch, I have to say - that you can't actually ski?'

'Steve...' she exclaimed with a hiss. The flush on Roger's face in response to that name confirmed what she already knew. That horrible man had taken his revenge on her, as promised.

'The source is irrelevant, Lola. What it boils down to are the rules. And the rules state that you have to be able to ski to work here. I can't turn a blind eye to this flagrant disregard for our most basic requirement, despite your sterling work so far.'

Lola sat, stunned, licking her lips nervously. Her worst fears were coming true and she could not let that happen. Not now, when she was so close to achieving her goal. Putting on her most innocent expression, she said sweetly, 'I really don't know where… *this person* got that idea. Nothing could be further from the truth.' She stood up. 'In fact, if there's nothing else, I was about to get in a swift run down the black slope before tonight's ceremony.'

Looking delighted, Roger stood and beamed at her. 'Oh, that's such a relief. Such a relief. I was worried I was going to have to let you go!'

'You have nothing to worry about, Roger. Why don't you go and get yourself ready for tonight, so you can look your best for Belinda?'

'No, no.' he said, coming around the desk and patting her shoulder. 'I think you have the best idea to kill some time. Why don't I join you? I'll meet you by the lifts in, say, half an hour?'

She nodded dumbly and stumbled out of the office. What on earth had she done?

Chapter Thirty

By the time Luka got back to Loveland, it was the afternoon, and the wind was picking up again. Dark clouds rolled across the sky with a promise of more snow to come. It had taken several hours for his truck to be unearthed from its snowy casing, and despite being ploughed, the highway was still treacherous and the going tough and tortuously slow.

Although he was desperate for a hot shower, his most pressing need was to find Lola. He parked up and trotted down the path to the village, pausing briefly to admire the tree in the square. Everybody had obviously been very busy while he was off on his misadventure. He also knew that somewhere on the complex was Belinda. It was only a few hours before the ceremony, so she must be here by now. He still didn't know how he would react if he saw her, and his eyes raked over every passer-by, fearful she would appear.

When he reached the offices, there was no one there, and he stood for a moment, wondering where on earth she could be. She had to be pretty busy with tonight's big event, so she could be anywhere he realised. He could search around the village and miss her at every turn. Deciding his best cause of action was to go home and get his phone charged up so he could reach her directly, he reversed his steps through the village and went back to his cabin.

He plugged his phone in and jumped into the shower to wash away the stink of the last 24 hours. When he was done, he dressed quickly and towelled his hair dry as he walked back into the living area to check if he had received any messages during his absence. His heart thumped when he saw the missed calls from Lola and the message icon. Listening to her voicemail, the pain and worry in her voice shot anguish through him and he was ashamed to be its cause.

Immediately, he tried to call her, but her phone was off. Frowning, he typed out a quick message letting her know he was back and that he wanted to see her urgently. At a loss for what else to do, he lay on the couch to rest. He was exhausted and needed to close his eyes for a while, but a notification on his phone jerked him upright again. Glancing at the screen, he saw it was just Roger, posting on Instagram again. He was about to toss his phone to one side in disgust when the wording caught his attention.

Letting off some steam before the big event tonight and hitting the slopes with our Events Organiser!!!

#workhardplayhard #loveland

He swiped it open, and there, looking absolutely terrified in that ridiculous pink suit, was Lola. They were standing by the chairlifts, Roger beaming away as usual. Lola was clutching her skis in front of her as if her life depended on it, her face a rictus of fear.

'*Merde*! What the hell does she think she is doing?' Standing abruptly, he spun around a couple of times, unsure what to do next, before grabbing his coat and running as fast as he could back down into the village. The skies were so cloud-laden it cast a dull light over everything, but the square was already busier than usual with guests arriving to claim their spot for tonight's big event.

Luka pushed his way through the growing crowd and spotted Tash. Grabbing her arm, he spun her around. 'Have you seen Lola?'

Her startled face creased into a frown. 'No, I've just come down. I haven't seen her since this morning, thankfully.'

Ignoring the barbed comment, he continued urgently. 'We have to find her. I think she's about to do something stupid!'

Tash gave a brittle laugh. 'Oh, my perfect sister never does anything stupid.'

Wordlessly, he pulled out his phone and showed her the picture, watching as her face fell and understanding dawned.

'Oh my God, what is she doing? She can't possibly think she can ski down a black run?'

'Apparently, she thinks she can. We have to stop her!'

'Well, they're going to close the lifts shortly. That bad weather is coming in again and we want to make sure everyone is off the slopes before it hits.'

Luka had to fight the rising tide of panic that was threatening to engulf him. His worst nightmares were coming to life. Seeing his face, Tash snapped into action.

'Hold on a minute, let me see if I can find them.'

She pulled the walkie talkie from her belt, pressing the button as she held it up to her face. 'Tash to Green's, Tash to Green's. Anyone spotted Roger and Lola heading up?'

There was a hiss of static and a distant voice came through. 'That's a negative, Tash.'

Nodding as if that made sense, she repeated the call to the Blue run lift operators. When she received the same response, she looked at Luka in horror.

'Maybe they've changed their minds? They might have thought better of it and we'll find them in the bar,' she said, her voice tinged with doubt. Before he could say anything, the handset crackled again.

'Hi Tash, it's Ben. I saw them not long ago. They're heading north to hit Patrol Bowl.'

Tash lowered her hand and stared at Luka, fear etched on her face. 'There's no way she can handle that run. She's going to kill herself,' she said hoarsely. 'We have to go after them.'

Luka staggered back, almost crumpling to the ground as fear flooded him, and his legs gave way. Tash's hand shot out and grasped the front of his coat, holding him up.

'Luka, I need your help to cover the ground. You have to come up there with me.'

Chapter Thirty-One

Lola's legs felt like jelly, and the tremor of her hands made it difficult to secure her helmet. Roger was babbling away. He hadn't stopped chattering the entire way up on the lift, despite her monosyllabic responses. Seemingly oblivious to her fear, he grinned at her. 'Time for another selfie,' he leaned over and snapped her tortured expression before she had time to smile for the camera, then zipped his phone safely back into a pocket in his suit.

'Shall we?' he asked, taking his stance, gazing keenly down the sheer face of the mountain.

'After you, boss,' she said, relieved when he didn't argue. With a quick jump, he shot down the mountain, zigzagging with expert ease. She stared after him, wondering how the hell she had landed in this position. The wind whipped her hair and the turbulent clouds looked close enough that she could reach out and touch them. She watched as a couple of other skiers arrived and followed Roger's path with the same zigzag swoops before heading down in a straight line. An idea sparked. There was no way she could follow them.

But maybe, just maybe, she could go from side to side like that and work her way down the run?

She focused her gaze and plotted her first two points before tentatively pushing off at a shallow angle so as not to pick up too much speed. Relieved when she drew to a stop at the first point, she awkwardly shuffled around and set off for the next, trying to keep out of the way of the enthusiastic skiers hurtling down the slope. She painstakingly made her way down, stopping after a while to catch her breath. This was exhausting.

A glance back up told her she had barely covered any distance at all and tears pricked her eyes. How on earth was she going to manage this? The slope seemed to go on forever, and it was getting darker and colder by the minute. Her fear made her sweat more than the exertion and the icy wind took advantage, freezing her to the bone despite her efforts to make some inroads.

It started to snow, thick flurries whirling around her, reducing her visibility. Hope sprung up. Maybe this was her chance to escape? If the weather was this bad, she could arguably make her way back up to the lift and get back to the safety of the village. She could claim disappointment if anyone asked, while warming up in front of the fire with some hot chocolate. Spirits lifted, she took off her skis, and began trudging back up the mountain, glancing up every now and again to keep the lines of the lift in sight. There didn't seem to be any more skiers charging down, so that was one less thing to worry about.

Pausing to move her skis to the other shoulder, she looked up again. She was closer now and could see the silhouettes of the chairs overhead. A howling gust of wind nearly blew her over, and she stumbled. Regaining her balance, she glanced up again just in time to see the lifts shudder to a halt. Lola stared in disbelief, willing them to start up again, but they remained resolutely still.

'Nooooo!' she screamed to the empty mountainside and sank to her knees with tears rolling down her face. Another blast of wind brought her to her senses, and she struggled to her feet, hoisting her skis back on her shoulder. Despairingly, she turned and forced herself to restart the journey back down the slope.

A few steps further, she stopped and chucked the skis and poles to one side with a triumphant yell. 'Ha!' she cried, happy at least to be rid of the dreaded encumbrances, then carried on her way. Half walking, half sliding, her progress seemed to be quicker than her previous attempt. Trying not to envision the enormity of the journey in front of her, she picked out landmarks to aim for. A desolate rock, a clump of lonely trees, anything that would make her feel like she was getting somewhere.

Her thoughts drifted to her sister. Who would look after her if she didn't make it down? And her grandparents? Shaking away these ghastly thoughts, she tried thinking about Luka instead. Well, the good bits at least. The warmth of his kisses, the way he smiled, his blue eyes dancing with delight. She had to make it down, if only to see him again. Her boots slid out from under her and she tumbled, rolling down the steep incline, smacking her head against a rocky outcrop. *Thank God I still have my helmet on,* she thought as stars span around her head. Dazed, she pulled herself up, looking around, unsure for a minute which way to go.

The weather was getting worse, and she could barely see more than a few feet ahead. Her boots sinking deep into the snow made it tough going as she trudged onwards. The wind was whipping her from every angle with angry blasts, and she realised she had no hope of making it down in these conditions. A clump of trees ahead offered the only possible shelter on the stark mountainside, so she headed towards them, thinking about waiting it out until the storm died down a little.

Sinking to the ground with her back against one of the trunks, she scrunched up as small as possible, trying to keep in some heat. The wind was still whistling between the trees, but she had some protection from the snow. Bone weary and miserable, her head sank to her chest, and she closed her eyes, praying for this nightmare to be over.

Chapter Thirty-Two

'I can't. I can't go up there,' Luka whispered in horror.

'Don't be ridiculous,' Tasha snapped at him. 'My sister is in danger, and I need as many people up there as possible.' She looked across the street and saw the hire shop. 'You wait there. I'll get Steve to come and help.' She legged it across and ran into the store. The bell sounding as she shoved open the door caused Steve to jump away from the girl he was with, but not before Tash saw what was going on.

'Tash, good to see you,' he lied smoothly, rushing over to her.

'She was right, wasn't she?' she demanded angrily. 'Lola was right when she said you were seeing other women?'

He glanced guiltily across at the girl who was watching the exchange with a frown. 'Come on, Tash, no need to be like that.'

With a snort, she glared at him. 'Listen, that's not important right now. I need volunteers to help me up on Patrol Bowl to find any stragglers.'

He looked at her in disbelief. 'If you think I'm going up there in this weather, you've got another thing coming!'

'Steve, I need your help. Lola is up there.'

Shaking his head, he walked away from her, looking back with a smirk. 'It serves her right.'

Dumbfounded, she ran out of the shop, back to where Luka was still standing, immobilised. Ben's voice crackled over the airwaves. 'Hey Tash, just confirming we've closed the lifts. I'm back at base now.'

Luka jolted out of his trance at this news. 'Tell him to wait there and be ready to go again. I'm going to get my gear, I'll meet you there.' He ran through the village, shoving people out of his way, desperate to get back to his cabin. Flying through the door, he pulled on his snowsuit and grabbed his equipment, pausing to pick up a backpack and blindly stuffing supplies into it from the back of his truck on his way back out.

Lola's in trouble, Lola's in trouble, pulsed through his brain in an urgent tattoo as he pounded back down the path towards the base of the lifts. When he arrived, panting, Tash was there talking to Ben and Roger, heads together. She looked up, white faced, as he skidded to a halt next to them.

'As far as we can tell, she's still up there,' she told him in a stilted voice. 'Roger says when he left, he thought she was right behind him, but he hasn't seen her since.' She gave a hiccup and covered her face with her hand, trying to hold it in. Ben moved over and put a protective arm around her. She took a deep breath. 'OK, here's the plan. Luka, you and I will head up. Ben, you run the lift until the rest of the crew gets back, then get as many people as are willing to come up and help with the search. Roger, call mountain rescue and have them on standby, just in case.'

The two men nodded and dispersed, leaving Luka to follow Tash onto the platform and wait for the lifts to start. He stood resolutely, staring ahead, flinching when the whir of machinery started up. Cold sweat was dripping down his back, and adrenaline was spiking through him in waves, making him want to vomit.

'You OK?' Tash asked, glancing at him.

'No,' he replied grimly, still staring straight ahead.

'The others will be here soon. You don't have to do this, you know?'

He finally met her concerned eyes and grimaced. 'Oh yes, I do.'

The chairs pulled around and swept them up. Luka banged the safety bar shut and closed his eyes. The falling sensation he had been avoiding for so long struck a chord of fear so deep he wanted to scream. His heart was pounding as he clutched onto the bar for dear life. The only thing keeping him sane was the fact that Lola needed him and that was bigger than the panic and fear pulsing through him.

A gust of wind buffeted them. The chair rocked, and he whimpered, trying to keep control. He felt Tash lay a supportive hand over his and he took deep, steadying breaths, keeping his eyes steadfastly closed until he heard her say, 'we're nearly there.'

He cracked open one eye and saw the terminal approaching, shuffling upright as he prepared to get off. When he hit the snow, he automatically slid away, years of ingrained experience making him move. He slid to a halt and pulled the straps of his poles over his wrists before glancing up at Tash, who was doing the same.

'Let's go and find Lola,' he said determinedly. She gave a grim nod, handed him a walkie talkie, and they both pushed away, following the path to the top of the slope.

Chapter Thirty-Three

Lola was struggling to stay awake. The continual shivering had stopped and every time she tried to think about doing something to get out of this predicament, the thoughts just slipped frustratingly away. Her head dropped to her chest, jolting her back into awareness, and she looked around, trying to remember where she was for a moment. The snowfall had eased up a bit, and she wondered idly if she should try to continue down the mountainside as her eyes fluttered closed again.

'You have to stand up, *Mija*,' a voice from her past whispered into her ear, and abruptly she was blinded by sunshine. The memory of warm sand under her feet and the smell of the ocean made her smile.

'*Mamita?*' she called out, lifting herself up, trying to follow the sound of the voice. Pushing up with her hands, the ground was disconcertingly cold, and a thought was nagging at her, but she couldn't grasp it. She was almost on her feet when she stumbled back onto her knees and fell forward, swiftly losing consciousness again.

Luka and Tash had split up, taking different routes down the slope but keeping in constant communication. The light was failing, and Luka was frantic, but trying to be systematic in his search. *I have to find her*, he thought desperately as he slid to a stop at the next ridge, eyes sweeping from left to right, searching every inch of his surroundings. Something caught his eye, sticking out of the snow, and he pushed off and aimed for it. He grasped the ski sticking up and wrestled it out, confirming what he already knew. It was Lola's. He dug around urgently, but all he found was the other ski and her poles.

'Tash,' he called over the handset. 'I've found her boards, but no sign of her yet.'

'Oh, God, OK. Keep going. I'm heading over now.'

The snow was easing off but had obliterated any trace of her path, and he scanned the hill, trying to second guess which way she would have gone on foot. Adjusting his backpack, he pushed off again, hoping he was going in the right direction. As he slipped down the hill, his eyes glanced over to a group of trees almost completely cloaked in snow, a flash of colour drawing his attention and he skewed to a halt. Never had he been so pleased to see that revolting pink suit of hers. He unclipped his skis and raced over, calling her name. Falling to his knees next to her, horrified to see she was face down in the snow, he flipped her over. She was like a pale rag doll.

'Lola! Lola!' Her eyelids fluttered and relief flooded through him. She was still alive... for now.

'I've got her, Tash, just past marker 24. We're going to need the airlift.'

A hiss of static preceded Tash's sob across the airwaves as she tried to control her voice. 'I hear you, Luka. Putting in the call now.'

Chucking the handset on the ground, he shrugged off the backpack, emptied out its contents and unfurled the sleeping bag. He knew he had to get her out of her wet clothes and warm her up as quickly as possible, but hesitated for a moment before unzipping her suit. She groaned softly as he manhandled her into the bag. He ripped open the thermopad packs and stuffed them in there before removing her helmet and zipping the bag up tightly until it fully enclosed her with just her nose peeking out.

Luka positioned his back against a tree trunk, pulled her until her head rested on his lap, then rifled through the pile of equipment to find the torch. Turning it on and jabbing it into the snow with the beam pointing skywards, he hoped it was strong enough to help the rescuers locate them.

A short while later, Tash came swooping down the hill, veering towards them when she caught sight of them. 'How is she?' she called as she came to a halt, unclipping her skis, dropping down next to them.

'She's hanging in there, I think. It's hard to tell.' He was staring down at her anxiously, absently rubbing his cheek. She placed a hand on his arm to still the motion.

'My sister is a fighter, Luka. She always has been. She'll be fine,' Tash declared vehemently. He looked at her and saw the uncertainty in her eyes, and nodded with a smile. 'Of course she will.'

Tash settled next to him, laying a protective hand on the sleeping bag, and glanced around at the contents of his bag on the ground. 'How come you had all this stuff? Are you some kind of secret emergency rescue dude on the quiet?'

Luka chuckled. 'I'm not usually this well prepared for emergencies, but thankfully I know someone who is.'

'Well, whoever it is deserves a medal,' Tash grinned. She cocked her head to one side. 'I think I can hear them.'

Luka strained his ears and heard a recognisable whomp-whomp sound of a helicopter approaching. He grabbed the torch from the snow and shoved it at her.

'Go and wave that at them!'

She jumped up and did what he said, dancing around like a lunatic. As the helicopter approached, the updraft from the blades whipped the snow around them and he bent to cover his face and protect Lola from the blizzard. Shielding his eyes with a hand, he watched as they lowered two flight paramedics to the ground, then the helicopter swooped off.

Feeling helpless, he stood with Tash, looking on as they checked her vitals and strapped Lola into the stretcher, calling for the helicopter to return. They moved her into position, pulling the winch hook into place when it was lowered and clipping it onto the stretcher.

'We'll have to come back for you two,' one paramedic shouted over the noise of the blades, and they watched as they swung her into the sky and hoisted her into the helicopter. The silence was deafening when it left. Luka staggered back against a tree, weak at the knees, the adrenaline that had been keeping him going seeping away.

'You did good, Luka,' Tash said, coming over and giving him a hug. 'Real good.'

'I only hope it was enough,' he said quietly, staring up at the sky.

Chapter Thirty-Four

'All signs indicate she is responding well. At her age, with no underlying conditions, she'll be up and around before you know it. She's a very lucky young lady'

'Thanks, Doc.'

Lola was struggling to make sense of where she was. She was wonderfully warm, but the constant beeping in the background and the quiet conversations going on around her were confusing. The sound of her sister's voice gave her something familiar to latch on to.

'Tash?' she called hoarsely as her eyes flickered open, briefly taking in the unfamiliar surroundings before her sister's strained face hovered above her and smiled gently.

'Hey, welcome back.'

Her muddled thoughts solidified, and her dark eyes widened in shock. 'Where am I?'

'You're in the clinic, Lola. We had to medivac you off the piste. It was all quite dramatic.'

'Shame I missed it,' Lola replied with a weak laugh that turned into a cough as she tried to sit up.

Tash helped her up, adjusting the pillows behind her before holding a plastic cup of water to her lips. She took a couple of sips, then let her head fall back feebly with a sigh, her mind going over the events that had occurred... when?

'How long have I been in here?'

'A couple of hours,' Tash smiled at her, brushing a strand of hair behind her ear, then resting her hand on Lola's arm. 'You gave us quite a scare, you know?'

'Probably not as much as the scare I gave myself! How did they find me?'

'*They* didn't. It was Luka.'

A jolt of surprise ran through her, her thoughts a twisted jumble as she tried to get her head around it.

'Luka came back?'

'Yup. Not only did he come back, but he came with me to search for you. In fact, if it wasn't for him, I might still be looking for you.'

Tash's face screwed up in an expression that Lola knew meant that her sister was barely keeping her emotions at bay. Lola lifted her free hand, ignoring the tug of the IV, and placed it on hers to give it a reassuring squeeze as she let this nugget of information settle.

'He went up? Up on the chairlift?'

Tash gave a low giggle. 'I thought he was going to pass out or chuck up over me, but yes, he did. That man of yours is pretty brave, I'd say.'

Lola suddenly felt even warmer than before. Those words, *that man of yours*, igniting a spark of hope in her.

'You think he's mine?'

Tash grinned, shaking her head disparagingly at her. 'Are you crazy? He completely freaked out when he knew you were in trouble, he was like a man possessed.'

'I didn't think he'd ever want to talk to me again, let

alone see me,' Lola said in amazement. Another memory surfaced, and she stared at Tash. 'For that matter, I didn't think you would either.'

'Lola, you are my sister. I will always end up talking to you, no matter how much you interfere in my life. And anyway, you were right about Steve,' she finished with a scowl of distaste. She sighed. 'What I ever saw in that man, I'll never know. I'm sorry I didn't listen to you, Sis.'

'When do you ever?' Lola laughed as Tash nodded acceptance of this fact. 'The ceremony! I've missed it. Did everything go OK?'

'Back in work mode immediately, what are you like? But yes, it went fine. According to Ben, there was an enormous crowd and the local TV station covered it, so you got the news footage you wanted. I asked him to film it for you, just in case you wanted to see Roger nearly wetting himself with excitement when Belinda gave him a kiss on the cheek at the end!'

Lola laughed, 'Oh my, I bet that's gone up on Instagram.'

'You know it, took about five seconds. He's thrilled, it's got a gazillion likes.'

'Well, at least something good came out of all this. Has he said anything about me getting stuck up there? Does he know I can't ski?'

Tash shook her head. 'I've no idea what he thinks went on. He was just concerned about you when I spoke to him earlier. In fact, I should go call him and let him know you're back in the land of the living.'

Tash rose, taking her phone out of her pocket. 'Besides, there's someone else waiting to see you,' she added with a grin. 'He refused to go home. He's just been waiting out in the corridor, growling at the doctors and nurses, telling them how to do their jobs.'

Lola's heart rate spiked, the machine standing next to the bed announcing it for all the world to hear, and Tash laughed. 'I'll let him know he can come in,' she said, walking towards the door.

'Tash,' Lola called, and her sister turned to look at her. 'I heard Mum. I swear I heard her voice when I was up there, telling me to get up, to keep moving.'

Her sister's eyes glazed with tears as she stared at her, and she gave a sniff. 'Sounds about right,' she said with a watery smile and walked out the door.

Lola rested back against the pillows, shifting to get comfortable, trying to take in everything that her sister had told her. She was exhausted, but the thought of her next visitor had her fizzing with excitement.

Luka had come back, and then he had overcome his fears to go up the mountain to rescue her. That had to mean something, right?

Chapter Thirty-Five

Luka leapt out of his seat like a scalded cat when Tash came out of the room. 'How is she?' he demanded, rushing over to her.

'She's awake, mostly lucid, and thrilled to know you are here. I told her you'd be in to see her.'

He shook his head. 'Non, I just wanted to wait... wait until I knew she was OK. I'm sure I am the last person she wants to see.'

Tash let out a dramatic sigh, throwing her hands in the air. 'I swear, I'm going to bang your heads together if you two don't sort yourselves out. She loves you and you love her. How difficult is that to understand?' she asked impatiently. 'Now get your butt in there and let my sister know how you feel about her!'

Tash walked down the hall, leaving Luka open-mouthed, staring after her. Love? Was this horrible crushing fear he'd been feeling the last few hours... love? The thought that he might lose Lola had been overpowering anything else. Not caring enough to dwell on the fact that Belinda was in town, or that he had, after eight long years, managed to get back on a chairlift. Just Lola.

He turned and looked at the door, took a deep breath, then walked in. Her eyes were closed and Lola looked like a child laying there. The various wires she was hooked up to made her look younger, more fragile. He gazed at her for a moment, taking in her dark lashes, the delicate curve of her cheek, her hair fanned out on the pillows.

'Are you going to stand there staring at me like some moronic Disney prince or are you gonna cut to the action?'

He blinked in shock, he'd thought she was asleep. 'What?'

Smiling, she opened her eyes, and his heart swelled to see the familiar glimmer of teasing there. He returned her smile and walked to the side of the bed, looking down at her adoringly. 'I'm glad to see you are feeling better, but I'm still not sure what you mean?'

'In the films, when the prince comes to save the sleeping princess, he has to kiss her.'

'But you're already awake...' he said, confusion wrinkling his brow.

'Luka, will you just get down here and kiss me?' she demanded.

And he did. Bending down to reach her, he gently and carefully placed his lips on hers, trying to let her know with this one touch everything he felt about her. When he straightened, he pulled up a chair to sit next to her, gripping her hand.

'You went up on the chairlift,' she stated, her eyes searching his face.

'I had no choice. Some silly woman decided to go far beyond her level of competence and got stuck,' he snorted.

'But you had a choice. You could have let someone else rescue that silly woman.'

He shook his head at her, his eyes crinkled up as he grinned. 'Non. I did not have a choice. Finding you was more important than anything else in the world.' He looked deep into eyes and added, 'it still is.'

He sat back a little, laughing. 'Are you blushing?'

'Not at all,' she insisted. 'It's these heat pad thingies they've got strapped to me.' They both looked up as a nurse came bustling in.

'How are you doing, Lola? The colour seems to be returning to your face.'

She shot Luka a look to stifle his chortles before answering. 'I'm feeling much better, thank you. How long do I need to be hooked up to this stuff?'

'Well, let me just check a few things and we'll see how we're doing,' the nurse answered, efficiently taking her blood pressure and checking her stats against her chart. 'It seems like everything is where it should be. I'll let the doctor know. He's doing his rounds shortly and once he gives the ok, we can unhook you.'

The room was silent when the nurse left, apart from the reassuring steady beat of her heart monitor. Luka was struggling to find the words that he needed to say to her. He desperately wanted her to understand. Dr Phillips's words came back to him. *It's best to start at the beginning.*

So he told her about his life before the accident, the work and the training that led to his success. He told her about his trainer Hank, who'd become like a father to him. About being swept off his feet by Belinda, who was so beautiful and successful in her own right and about his friendship with his teammate Marcel.

He faltered when he got to the day of the accident, his

face pale as he began to describe cajoling Marcel to go up for one last run when he really didn't want to.

'You don't have to tell me,' Lola told him earnestly. 'I've seen the news reports. I know what happened.'

But he took another deep breath and continued quietly, laying it all bare so she knew every horrible thing that he had thought since that day.

'So, now I am seeing Dr Phillips,' he finished up. 'He tells me I have PTSD, which is why I have struggled to be, er, well…'

'Nice? Social? Friendly? Normal?' she grinned at him and he laughed, relief that she finally knew everything coming out in hearty chuckles.

'I am very glad that none of that seemed to put you off one little jot.'

'I had to put up with you. I needed to learn how to ski.' Lola's face fell, and he knew she was worrying about Roger and her job.

'Don't worry, Lola, everything will turn out for the best,' he told her, grasping her hand tighter to comfort her.

The door opened again, this time revealing the doctor, closely followed by Tash. He picked up her chart from the end of the bed and slid his glasses onto his nose. 'Ms Sanchez?' He smiled at her. 'The nurse tells me you are doing well and are quite keen to be unhooked from our paraphernalia.'

'I sure am,' said Lola, pushing herself upright. She looked at Tash inquiringly. 'How was Roger?'

Her sister smiled reassuringly. 'He was fine, thrilled to hear you're on the mend and said he'll have a good 'ol chat with you when you get back.' Seeing Lola's face she rushed on, 'I don't think he meant anything by that. Just the usual Jolly Roger stuff.'

Luka's heart went out to her. Despite Lola's effort to look calm, he could see she was anything but, and he hoped against hope that Roger wouldn't fire her when she got back. He didn't want to lose her again.

Chapter Thirty-Six

They kept Lola in overnight for observation, despite her pleas to be released. All she wanted to do was get out of here and back to Loveland to see if she still had a job. But she had to admit she was exhausted, although whether it was from her ordeal or the constant worry, she didn't know.

'You should go,' she told Luka, who hadn't moved from the chair next to her. 'There's no point in both of us being stuck in here all night.'

He leaned forward and kissed her. 'I'm not letting you out of my sight. You're not to be trusted by yourself.'

She tutted crossly at him, but her heart was singing at his words. She still couldn't believe he was here, and he loved her. So he stayed, and they talked quietly into the night until she dozed off, unable to fight it any longer. When she woke up with a start in the early hours of the morning, he was still there. He'd fallen asleep, his head resting on their clasped hands. She stroked the side of his face with her free hand, falling back asleep, content.

It was late afternoon, the next day when they finally let her leave, insisting she sit in a wheelchair until she reached Luka's truck.

'I'm fine!' she scowled. 'I don't see why they are making me sit in this.'

'Lola, you've been through a lot. Give your body some time to recover, please,' Luka told her patiently as he lifted her into the passenger seat. Lola felt the relief of being free dwindle as they approached Loveland. The inevitable chat with Roger was stressing her out. She didn't have any idea what she would do next if he upheld this ridiculous rule about skiing.

When they pulled up in the parking area next to the cabins, a message came through from Roger, asking her to join him in the meeting hall once she had got herself settled. *Well, this is it*, she thought to herself. *The end of my master plan.* She messaged back to say she would be there in an hour. She desperately wanted a quick wash and change before she faced him.

Swinging her legs round and slipping to the ground, she had to steady herself against the body of the truck. She was weaker than she realised. Luka came around without a word, slipping his arm around her waist and supporting her until they got into her cabin. Grateful for his unobtrusive support, she smiled at him as he lowered her to the couch.

'Thank you, Luka. I'm just going to have a quick wash and change into something a little more business-like,' she told him, waving her hand at the sweatpants and hoodie combo Tash had dropped off for her this morning. 'And then I will go and face Roger.'

A secretive smile flickered across his face. 'I'm sure there is nothing to worry about. I'll come with you.'

'No. There's no need. I appreciate your support, but I have to face this by myself.'

'Lola Sanchez, you are going to let me help you whether you like it or not,' he said sternly, making her giggle.

'OK, OK. You can come over there with me, but I will go into the meeting alone.'

When Lola was happy with her appearance, they made their way slowly down to the village. They had cleared the paths after the big storm, but it was still slippery underfoot. She smiled when they reached the square. It looked wonderful with the tree lit up and all the decorations in place. *At least I got something right while I was here*, she thought sadly.

Her heart was pounding as she paused outside the door of the meeting room. Luka swept her into his arms and kissed her. 'Whatever happens, sweetheart, I'm here for you,' he whispered into her hair. Taking strength from him, she took a deep breath and opened the door.

'Surprise!' chorused the people in the room at top volume. She stood in shock, taking in the decorations and the big jaunty banner saying 'Welcome back, Lola.' The tables had been lined up along one side and were laden with food, paper plates, and cups, and there was a big pot of what smelled like mulled wine.

'What? What's all this?' she stuttered in amazement.

Tash ran over, grinning, and gave her a big hug. 'We just wanted to let you know how glad we all are that you are in one piece and back here with us,' she told her, pulling back and waving her arm at the rest of the crowd. And Lola could see she was right, it looked like the entire staff were here to celebrate her return. She could see Ben and the rest of the lift crew, the kids' entertainment team, and even Chad standing there grinning happily at her.

Momentarily overwhelmed by gratitude, her hand flew to her mouth, her eyes glistening with unshed tears. As she felt Luka's arm slip around her, she leaned into his support and plastered a smile on her face.

'Well, let's get this party started!'

They thrust a warming cup of mulled wine into her hands and she made her way around the room, chatting to everyone who had made her feel so welcome here. She hesitated when she got to Roger, but before she could say anything, he grabbed her in a bear hug.

'Good to have you back Lola, very good indeed,' he chirped happily. Surprised by his demeanour, she said tentatively, 'About the other day...'

'Yes, yes. Dreadful incident,' he interrupted her. 'Very dreadful, in fact,' he paused to take a sip of wine before continuing with a gleam in his eyes. 'I wouldn't be surprised if someone that had to go through a horrible thing like that didn't put skis on again. Not once. For the entire season,' he finished, waggling his eyebrows at her.

She wordlessly stared at him in amazement until Luka poked her in the ribs. 'Uh, yes. I fear you might be right,' she said breathlessly, happiness blooming through her. 'It will be heartbreaking not being up to skiing again, but what can I do?' Lola shrugged her shoulders. Roger leaned in and whispered with a wink, 'don't overdo it.'

She beamed at him, then looked around sharply, aware that someone was missing. 'Where's Steve?'

Roger blew out a breath. 'Ah, sadly, I had to let him go. It seems he was up to inappropriate things with some of our younger female guests.'

This came as no surprise to Lola, and she looked over to where her sister was standing. She was chatting happily with a group of the lift crew and Lola was glad to see Ben hovering right next to her, gazing at her with adoration.

'Can I have everyone's attention, please?' Roger called out, waiting until the chatter around the room subsided. 'I just wanted to thank you all for being here to welcome back our wonderful Events Coordinator, Lola.' They greeted this with whoops and cheers, and Lola ducked her head, embarrassed by the attention. 'As you know, Lola was, er, indisposed the other night, and didn't get to see the wonderful Lighting up Loveland ceremony that she had organised. So, I'm going to play it now so she can see how fantastic it was,' he beamed at the room. He fiddled with his laptop on the table behind him, calling out, 'can someone get the lights?'

She felt Luka still next to her as the scene began to play on the screen on the wall. She grasped his hand tighter, even though it was slick with sweat, as they watched the event. *There was an enormous crowd*, she thought distantly, more concerned with how Luka was going to cope. The crowd in the square erupted into applause as Belinda strode onto the stage towards a visibly animated Roger. There she was. *The woman who broke this man's heart so cruelly*, Lola thought as she watched the event play out. It was thankfully brief, Roger pausing it on the moment when Belinda kissed his cheek, just in case anyone missed it. The lights came back on, the chatter starting up again, and Lola turned to Luka.

'How are you doing?' she asked, looking at him intently, trying to gauge his reaction. He was still staring at the screen, but when he looked down at her, he had a puzzled smile on his face.

'You know, I was dreading seeing Belinda again, but it was fine,' he said in wonderment. 'I mean, all I felt was a pang of sadness, but not anything like I expected. I thought it would drive me crazy.'

She reached up to kiss him. 'Well, maybe that's because you have something else to worry about now?' she asked with a grin.

'You mean someone?' he grinned back at her. 'Someone irritatingly persistent and absolutely terrible at skiing?'

'Yes, that someone,' she replied, and kissed him again.

Epilogue

Christmas day dawned bright and sunny, the storms of the last few weeks finally clearing, and the sunlight glinted off of the frosty boughs of the trees that lined the path. The Sanchez sisters chatted happily as they made their way to the hall for the staff Christmas lunch Lola had organised. Tash was holding a big tray of Conchas, the sweet traditional bread that had always been part of their festive table. As the staff comprised a mishmash of nationalities and traditions, Lola had decided to make it a potluck, asking everyone to bring something from their culture. Lola had made tamales. She had called her grandmother to get the exact recipe that their family had used for generations, and the smell of them brought back memories of home.

When they arrived, her eyes immediately sought Luka, and she saw him sitting at the table in the corner, chatting happily with Ben and some of the other lift crew. She watched him for a moment. Seeing him looking so relaxed and happy was the best Christmas present she could wish for. He still had a long way to go - Dr Phillips had made that quite clear when she had joined them for one of his sessions. But opening himself up to help had already made a tremendous difference, and the Loveland team were doing everything they could to support him.

As if sensing her gaze, his eyes flicked up and locked with hers, a broad smile appearing on his handsome features, and he stood and came over.

'Merry Christmas, Lola,' he said, enfolding her in his arms and kissing her. A whoop and catcalls erupted around the room, and they pulled apart reluctantly.

'I have a surprise for you,' she whispered to him.

'Oh, yes?' he grinned so cheekily that Lola flushed.

'Look behind you,' she said, pushing his chest, and he turned and stared in amazement.

'Hank!' he cried, and closed the gap quickly to embrace his old trainer for a long minute. 'What are you doing here?'

'Well, son. That little lady of yours convinced me that I'm the best family that you've got, and that's what Christmas is for, right?' Hank grinned up at him. Shaking his head in wonderment, Luka looked back at her, the joy on his face worth every penny of the plane ticket to get Hank here.

They all settled at the tables to enjoy the smorgasbord of food on offer. The wine was flowing and the volume of chatter increased over the festive music playing in the background, until Roger stood, clinking his glass to get their attention.

'I just wanted to say a few words,' he told the expectant faces as he beamed round at them. 'First off, a big thank you to Lola for organising this.' A cheer went up around the tables, and he waited until it subsided before carrying on. 'Secondly, I wanted to thank you all for being here. You guys are like a family to me, not just people who work for me. I thank my stars every day for the wonderful team we have here at Loveland. Merry Christmas, everyone,' he finished with a sniff, sitting back down to rowdy applause and cries of Merry Christmas.

Lola felt Luka take her hand. 'Will you come outside? I have something for you.'

Slightly perplexed, she followed him as he stood and led the way out into the sparkling sunshine.

'So, what is it?' she demanded, looking around. He grinned at her impatience and pulled an envelope out of his jacket. Frowning, she fumbled it open, gasping when she saw the contents.

'You bought me a ticket to Cabo?'

Nodding, he smiled even further, reaching in to pull all the paperwork out. 'I bought *us* tickets to Cabo, for the end of the season.'

Awestruck, she looked at him, 'you want to come with me?'

'Lola Sanchez, if you think I am ever letting you out of my sight again, you are even more *loca* than your sister tells me you are!'

With that he kissed her, so deeply and soundly that she knew he meant every word, and she had finally found the one man who she wanted to make a part of her family.

More by Joy Skye

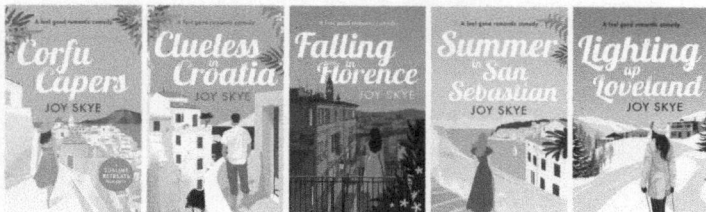

vinci-books.com/sublimeretreats

Follow the link to stay up to date with Joy Skye's new releases